Book Five
Dog-Gone Danger

Book Five
Dog-Gone Danger

Linda Joy Singleton

Albert Whitman & Company
Chicago, Illinois

To animal control officer, Stacey Vavzincak, and his daughter Savannah. And to my editor, Eliza Swift, who loves series books like I do.

Library of Congress Cataloging-in-Publication data is on file with the publisher.

Contents

Kelsey Case

Ms. Wirt's Third Period

Assignment: Essay on Irony

When Good Deeds Go Bad

The dictionary defines IRONY as a "state of affairs or an event that seems contrary to what one expects." And I know from real-life experience that you can do a good deed for someone else that causes something bad to happen to you.

I'm supposed to give an example to back up my statement, so I'll tell you something that happened a few weeks ago.

It started off with a good deed that was rewarded. After volunteering at a fund-raiser for the Humane Society, my father got a cool new job and a rent-free house big enough for my family plus our little kitten and big dog. We LOVED this wonderful house and hoped to live there for a long time.

But then I did a good deed. I helped my father's boss unmask a thief, find a lost emerald, and reunite with his missing family. Dad's boss was thrilled when his family wanted to move back into their home. Unfortunately, their home was our wonderful new house, so my family had to move out.

In conclusion, irony sucks. My reward for doing a good deed was eviction. Now my family is homeless. And it's all my fault.

- Chapter 1 -
Barking Mad

Piles and piles of smashed cars rise in metal hills as far as I can see. It's a graveyard where vehicles come to die, filled with broken glass, twisted bumpers, and rotting tires. The air is heavy with the stinky smells of oil, rubber, and other acrid odors I can't identify. Shadows shift, the afternoon sun glinting, and a rusting school bus turns into a lurking dragon with glowing headlight eyes.

Out there, hidden somewhere, are two boys.

"You can find them, Major," I say, gripping the leash tightly. I look down at the German shepherd who sits obediently beside me.

Major is probably smarter than most humans. His velvety brown ears are triangles of alertness, twitching slightly as he waits for my commands. He always seems to be listening, something we have in common. In my large family, I'm the quiet one who listens a lot. My ability to observe and lip-read is why my title in the Curious Cat Spy Club is Spy Specialist. Major may not be able to lip-read, but he used to be a search and rescue dog, so he has lots of cool skills—which is why I brought him to Pete's Pick and Pull, the local car graveyard.

There's a tap on my shoulder, and I turn to face my closest friend, Becca Morales. Her pink-streaked black hair is pulled back in a leopard-print bandanna that matches the stretchy tights below her black skirt. She's a talented fashion designer and makes most of her own clothes.

"Ready to start?" Becca asks, bending down to pat Major's head.

"Are you talking to Major or me?"

"Both!" Her dark eyes sparkle. "It'll be fun to see Major in action."

"I could use some fun." Sighing, I stare at a smashed-car tower. It sways even though there's no wind.

Becca's face softens, and she reaches out to squeeze my hand. "Don't think about your family."

I nod, relieved to escape my house...well, not really *my* house but my grandmother's. When Dad's boss, Mr. Bragg, asked us to move out of his cottage, he offered us a fancy suite in his castle until we could find a new house. My older brother and parents moved into the castle, but my twin sisters preferred to stay with friends. I think Bragg Castle is cool, but my dog and kitten had to stay with my grandmother, so that's where I went too. I was surprised when Mom joined me at Gran's a week later. I thought it was weird, but I've enjoyed sharing the guest room with her.

The search and rescue game was Becca's idea. When she found out Major was a trained rescue dog, she thought it would be fun to test his skills. Also, it'll test our CCSC spy skills. Our associate member, Frankie, suggested we use his uncle's wrecking yard, and he and Leo volunteered to hide. Becca and I are in charge of Major. The German shepherd is temporarily living with my grandmother while his elderly owner, Greta, is in the hospital. When she's well enough to come home, she'll take Major back.

"Doesn't Major need clothing from the boys to sniff?" Becca asks, shielding her eyes as she stares up at the panorama of wrecked vehicles. "I always thought SAR-trained dogs followed scented stuff to find missing people."

"They do, but according to Gran Nola, Major had training to locate people trapped in natural disasters. She said he is..." I try to think of the word my grandmother used. "Air trained."

"Oh, I've heard about that," Becca says. She lives on an animal sanctuary and is our CCSC animal expert and Social Contact Operative. She knows everything there is to know about animals.

"Major will ignore our scents because he can see us," I add. "But when he smells the boys, he won't see them, so he'll search until he finds them."

"Coolness." Becca's ponytail flops as she bounces eagerly on her sneaker toes. "Let's get started."

I reach around Major's blue collar and click off his leash. A thrill of excitement rushes through me as I say, "Major, find the boys!"

He just sits there, doing nothing.

"Let me try." Becca kneels beside the German shepherd. "Major, our club mates Leo and Frankie are lost somewhere out there. They need your help. Please find them."

But politeness doesn't seem to work either.

"Go!" I say firmly, giving Major a gentle push. "Find. The. Boys."

Major doesn't make a move.

"Now!" I shout. "Search!"

Major whines, looking up at me with liquid brown eyes. But the only movement he makes is to lick my arm.

Becca frowns. "Are you sure he's trained to find people?"

"Gran said Major rescued an entire family after an earthquake destroyed their home. I don't understand why he's sitting there doing nothing."

"He's retired now and old in dog years. He probably has arthritis." Becca runs her fingers across Major's black-and-tan fur. "He's getting gray around his muzzle too."

"But he rescued his owner and can keep up with me when I'm on my bike," I argue. "He's not too old. I think he's just being stubborn."

"Why is there a delay in the canine discovery experiment?" a familiar voice calls out. Leo Polanski, the CCSC's Covert Technology Strategist, strides toward us. He looks nice in a dark vest over a navy-blue shirt and pressed black slacks—like he's at a wedding instead of in a wrecking yard.

Becca wags her finger at Leo. "You were supposed to stay hidden."

"I did until nineteen minutes passed. Is there a problem?" Leo brushes dust off his vest. I notice that he's changed out of the dark leather shoes he wore in school today and into black-striped sneakers like mine.

"A Major problem." I frown. "He won't search."

"I wonder why he won't obey us," Becca says with a thoughtful look at the dog. "It could have something to do with his training. Maybe you're not using the right words."

"Like a magical spell?" I ask, thinking of my favorite fantasy novels. But I doubt fictional commands like *accio* or *mobiliarbus* will work on Major. Sighing, I click his leash back on his blue collar. "There's no point in hanging around here. I'm going home…I mean…to my grandmother's house."

"Yeah, we might as well leave." Becca sounds as disappointed as I feel. "Kelsey, I'll go with you to your grandmother's and stay until I have to go home for dinner if you'd like."

"Yeah, I would." I give her a grateful smile, then turn to Leo to ask if he wants to come with us.

But when I look at him, I catch him looking at me, and the words stick in my throat. Is there dirt on my face? Is my hair messy? Am I blushing? Ever since I went with Leo on his birthday trip to San Francisco, things have been weird between us.

"Um...go ahead." Leo takes a step back. "I-I have to find Frankie."

I peer around. "Is he still hiding?"

"Yes. And since he knows the best hiding spots, he said no animal or person could find him. But he can't elude me." Leo sweeps his gaze around the wrecking yard. "According to my calculations, and factoring in the direction Frankie took, he's in that school bus."

"It's like a giant metal monster," Becca says with a shudder.

I nod, remembering how I imagined it lurking like a dragon. "But I don't think that's where he's hiding." I point to the towering hill of cars. "I saw that huge pile sway."

Leo purses his lips skeptically. "It would take a tornado to move that mountain of metal."

"Or a boy using it as a hiding place," I suggest. "Check there for Frankie."

"Great observation, Kelsey," Leo says with a

grin that makes me grin too. We used to argue a lot, so his compliment feels weird. He stares like he's waiting for me to say something. My cheeks burn.

"We should go, Becca. Come on, Major." I jerk on the leash and quickly turn to flee the wrecking yard.

I immediately regret walking instead of biking. The mile walk didn't seem long coming from my grandmother's house. Now it seems like a marathon.

"Kelsey, slow down," Becca complains when she catches up with me. "Leo isn't watching anymore."

"I don't care what Leo does," I snap.

"You're so obvious." Becca grins as we fall into step, Major leading the way. "You've been crushing on Leo since you went on that date to San Francisco with him."

"It wasn't a date."

Becca giggles. "Okay, a not-date."

"He only invited me because he had an extra ticket to the World Robot Tournament."

"Also because he likes you lots," Becca says. "You two are so cute together."

I kick a rock across the sidewalk and into a ditch. "We are *not* together."

"Well, you should be. I know!" Becca snaps her

fingers, her purple nail polish glinting in the sun. "You should ask him to the Spring Fling dance."

"I can't." I pause. "He already asked me."

Becca's mouth falls open. "Seriously? And you're just now telling me this astounding news?"

"There was no reason to say anything because"—I stumble over uneven sidewalk—"I told Leo I needed time to think it over. Well, I have, and I'm not going."

"Why not?"

I don't want to keep secrets from Becca (except for other people's secrets, which I write down in my notebook of secrets), so I lead Major to a shady spot beside a stone wall. "I don't have anything formal to wear, and this is a terrible time to ask Mom to take me shopping. Besides I'm—"

"—afraid to admit you like Leo," Becca says with a knowing smile.

I'm saved from answering by a familiar whirring sound.

Spinning around, I stare as Leo zooms toward us on his gyro-board, a robotized skateboard that bends in the middle.

"Here comes your future dance partner," Becca teases, giving me a playful nudge.

"Becca!" I shoot her a murderous look. Just then, I'm jerked forward as Major barks and lunges on his leash. "Settle down, boy!"

"Need help?" Leo rolls up, circling to a stop so we're face-to-face.

"I got this under control." I grip the leash tightly to hold Major back, raising my voice to be heard over the barking. "Why aren't you with Frankie?"

Leo jumps off his gyro-board, grinning. "He stayed with his uncle. I switched to turbo speed to catch up with you."

I try to hide how pleased I am to see him, and I'm so focused on Leo that I don't notice the leash slipping from my fingers. Suddenly, I'm holding empty air. I spin around as a black-and-tan streak bolts across the road.

"Major! Come back!" I cry, then take off running. I keep shouting at Major, but he runs faster down the sidewalk.

Becca races beside me, but we can't outrun a German shepherd. Leo zooms ahead on his robotic skateboard, and I hope he can catch Major.

Leo is gaining on him, squatting on the gyro-board, his hand stretching for the leash. Closer, closer, almost there...

Major makes a sharp right. He lopes down a country road so rural there's no street sign. Becca and I catch up with Leo, who has stopped in the middle of the rutted dirt road. On either side of the road—and as far as the eye can see—are wheat fields.

"It's too bumpy for my gyro-board," Leo says with a frustrated frown. He tucks his remote in his pocket and carries the board.

"We have to keep looking." I press my lips, scanning the fields for rustling stalks of wheat or a glimpse of the German shepherd.

Becca shades her eyes to peer down the road. "This is a dead end. Major can't go too far."

"Unless he went through the fields." I cup my hands over my mouth and call out for Major again and again. Becca and Leo shout too.

We keep calling as we hurry down the road. Stalks of wheat rise higher than my head. Beyond the horizon of crops, the only visible building is a decrepit old barn that looks like a sneeze could knock it down.

My throat is sore from shouting by the time we reach the dead end. A padlocked metal gate has a sign warning, "Trespassers will be shot! Survivors will be shot again!" Beyond the gate, a narrow dirt road disappears into rolling hills. I look down in front of the gate. The ground is crisscrossed with tire tracks that look fresh, as if different vehicles have driven here recently. There are paw prints too, trailing beyond the gate.

I look up to see Major coming out of the barn.

He's carrying something in his mouth.

When I realize what, I gasp.

- Chapter 2 -
Buggy

Hurrying away from the barn, Major squeezes through a hole beneath the fence near the padlocked gate. With dark eyes shining proudly, he plops a tiny puppy into Becca's hands. It has oatmeal-brown fur, a squishy black face, and big, buggy eyes.

"A pug," Becca says.

"It's unusually minuscule for a canine," Leo observes as we close in around Becca. She snuggles the puppy to her chest.

"Even full-grown pugs only weigh about fifteen pounds, and this one is just a few weeks old. It's a"—Becca lifts the tail—"female. But why is she out here all by herself? Where's your mommy, little one?" she croons. The pug whimpers and buries her black nose in Becca's shirt.

Leo's gaze sweeps over rolling hills and wheat fields. "There are no dwellings except that barn where half of the roof has collapsed."

"Major seemed to know the puppy was there." I glance down at Major, who watches the puppy closely. "You really are a search and rescue dog, aren't you?"

"And a darned good one." Becca pats the German shepherd's head. "This pup wouldn't have survived much longer if Major hadn't found her."

"We should search the barn for clues." I rattle the padlock on the gate, wishing I had my key spider to pick the lock open.

Becca shakes her head. "If we go into the barn, the rest of the roof might fall on us. Besides, we need to leave so the pup can eat and drink."

I reach out toward Becca. "Can I hold her?"

"Sure." Becca gently sets the puppy in my hands.

The pug's little black face is so precious, with black eyes as round as marbles and soft dark-brown ears. She licks my hand, and it tickles. My heart totally melts. "When I looked through the lost-pet flyers Mom gave me this morning, only adult dogs were missing. No puppies."

Leo taps his chin thoughtfully. "So how did she get way out here?"

Becca's expression darkens. "Someone dumped her."

I suck in a breath. "That's heartless."

"Unfortunately, it happens a lot." Becca twists her pink-streaked ponytail and sighs. "Living at an animal sanctuary, I've seen people do horrible things to animals too many times."

"But why not give her away or sell her?" I cuddle the pup, rocking her like a mother comforting a child. "If she's a purebred, she's worth lots of money."

"Her markings *do* look purebred." Becca studies the puppy. "But if she wasn't abandoned, how did she get way out here? She's thin but otherwise in good shape, so she can't have been on her own for long."

"Someone must be missing her," I say. "When Mom gets home from work, I'll check the latest lost-dog reports." My mom is an animal control officer and often brings home missing-pet reports for us. I hug the trembling pup and never want to let her go. "I can take care of her until we find her owner."

"It's more logical for me to keep her," Leo says. "You already have two dogs and a kitten at your grandmother's house. I only have fish and a kitten."

"But she may need medical care and bottle-feeding." Becca pushes away her leopard-spotted bandanna as she leans in for a closer look. "She's dehydrated and probably isn't weaned. The best place for her is at the animal sanctuary where Mom and I can nurse her back to health."

Becca's right, and I can tell from Leo's expression that he knows it too. Reluctantly, I hold out the pug to Becca. But she shakes her head and takes Major's leash. "I'll walk Major, and you carry the pup. I know you want to."

"Thanks." I smile and cradle the tiny pup in my arms as we retrace our steps to the main road. The puppy licks my skin and wiggles her curly tail. "Her buggy eyes shine like she's thanking us for rescuing her."

"Buggy." Becca snaps her fingers. "That's what we'll call her."

"That's an inaccurate name. She's a canine, not an insect." Leo clicks his remote to a slow speed and rolls beside us, swerving around a pothole.

"But her eyes bug out funny." I pet the pup's soft tawny head. "Buggy, do you like your name?"

She licks me again, which seems like an overwhelming yes.

By the time we turn onto my grandmother's street, Buggy has fallen asleep in my arms. She's tiny like a fuzzy toy, and I wonder again how she got into that dilapidated barn. There were no homes or cars around—although the tire tracks by the locked gate were proof that someone had been there recently.

Was it the cruel person who dumped Buggy?

I'm reminded of when we found our three kittens in a dumpster and worked together to rescue them but couldn't take them to any of our homes. So we fixed up a hidden shack on Becca's property and cared for the kittens until we could keep them. We also formed the CCSC to help animals and solve mysteries. Will we be able to solve the mystery of Buggy?

When we turn the last corner, there's Gran Nola's dark-blue house. I check the driveway for Mom's animal control truck. *Drats*. Only Gran Nola's sporty convertible. Mom must be working late. I'll have to wait to ask her about Buggy.

"Gran Nola!" I call out as we enter the house. I hear music from the exercise room. My grandmother teaches yoga, although not usually this late in the afternoon.

The music abruptly stops, and Gran Nola steps out into the hallway, wearing purple capri tights and a black tank top. Sweat gleams on her face as she grins at us. "I thought I heard voices. I was trying out some new poses and...What is *that*?"

I proudly hold up the tiny puppy. "Buggy."

"Oooh, what an adorable pug." Gran scoops up the puppy from my arms and kisses her face. "Who does she belong to?"

"We have yet to determine that answer," Leo says.

"Major found her," I add, explaining how Major wouldn't play the search and rescue game but did a for-real search and rescue.

"This darling pup was abandoned?" Gran Nola asks.

"I think she was dumped," Becca says ominously.

"No!" my grandmother gasps. "That's despicable! Whoever did that should be shackled and dumped in a pit of rabid alligators."

"Reptiles aren't rabid," Leo says, his mind as quick as Google. "Rabies is a mammalian disease."

"A puppy dumper deserves worse anyway," Gran Nola says with a scowl as she turns toward me. "Kelsey, your mother will be very interested in this. She said there were disturbing things going on with animals in Sun Flower."

"What kind of things?" I take back the puppy from my grandmother and let Leo have a turn at holding her.

"You'll have to ask your mother." Gran pulls off her sweatband and finger combs her hair. "I'm surprised she isn't home yet."

I hear a whine from the backyard and watch Major scamper to the sliding-glass door. On the other side of the glass, my gorgeous dog, Handsome—a golden retriever and whippet mix—wags his tail eagerly.

"Handsome wants to play with Major," I say, smiling. When we first introduced the dogs to each other, I worried they wouldn't get along since Handsome is much younger than Major. But they quickly bonded over their love for Frisbees.

I cross the room and slide open the glass door. Handsome jumps excitedly, a Frisbee hanging from his mouth. Major races to join him in the backyard.

When I turn around, Becca is at the kitchen sink, pouring water into a bowl for Buggy. "I hope she's weaned." Becca places the bowl on the floor. "Bottle-feeding isn't hard, but it's a pain."

I hold my breath, watching the pup lean into the water dish. Her claws click on the tile as she sniffs the water. She snorts and backs away from the dish.

"She's not drinking," I say with a sigh.

Becca kneels and nudges Buggy. "Go on, girl. Sip the water," she croons, gently pushing Buggy's muzzle into the water. The puppy sputters and scampers across the kitchen.

But Becca doesn't give up. Murmuring soothing words, she eases the pup back to the dish. Becca dips her finger in the water and puts it up to the pup's mouth. Buggy sniffs, licks Becca's finger, and dips her whiskery nose into the dish. She sloppily laps water, splashing the floor and our sneakers.

"Coolness!" Becca beams.

"If only Major did what we wanted this easily," I say, glancing outside at the dogs playing tug-of-war with a Frisbee.

"It's odd that Major wouldn't search for you." My grandmother puts her hands on her hips, staring into the backyard with a thoughtful look. "It doesn't make sense. I've seen his medals and newspaper clippings."

"We told him to search," I say. "But he sat there like he didn't understand."

"While I was cramped in a car trunk for nineteen minutes," Leo complains.

"But he rescued Buggy," Becca points out, still kneeling beside the tiny dog on the floor. "Buggy wouldn't have lasted long out there alone. Major saved her life."

"I just remembered something Greta told me that might explain why he ignored your commands." My grandmother takes a dishrag off the counter and tosses it to Becca. "She said when Major went to work, he wore a tracking harness."

I glance into the backyard. "He's wearing a blue collar."

"So maybe that's why he didn't search for you," Gran Nola says. "When Major is at home, he's an off duty family dog. If you want him to work, he needs to wear his harness."

"Where is it?" I ask as Becca wipes the water off the floor.

"Good question." Gran Nola grabs the damp dishcloth that Becca hands her. "I'll ask Greta. I was planning on calling to check on her anyway."

"Thanks," I say. Footsteps sound outside the

front door. "Mom must be home!"

I rush to the door, eager to tell her everything that happened today. But when I open the door, Mom staggers in, clutching her thigh. A dark-red stain is splattered on her uniform.

Mom's been shot.

- Chapter 3 -
Risky Business

"Mom!" I rush forward and wrap my arms around her. "Are you okay?"

She winces. "I'll be fine once I shower and sleep."

"You're clearly *not* fine. You're going to the hospital right now," my grandmother says forcefully. "I can't believe you drove home instead of getting medical help. You must be in shock."

"I was shot…but not with a real gun." Mom points down to her leg. "This isn't blood. It's paint. I was hit with a paintball, and it stings like crazy."

Gran Nola and I sandwich Mom between us and ease her over to the soft leather recliner.

"How did it happen?" Gran Nola gently strokes Mom's brown hair.

My mother sucks in a deep breath. "It was supposed to be a routine call," she explains, leaning back in the recliner. "We received a biting report. Frankly, the neighbor deserved it. He was throwing rocks at the dog. And the dog's a toy poodle, so the bite barely broke the skin. But the dog's owner didn't have proof of a rabies vaccination, and the victim filed a complaint. So I had to take the poodle in for quarantine."

"Is that why the owner shot you?" Gran Nola guesses.

My mother bites her lip. "The owner, Mike, didn't give me any trouble. He knew he'd get the dog back once he found the vaccination documents. But as he handed the dog over, his daughter came running out of the house, sobbing hysterically. I thought she was holding a toy gun until a sharp pain blasted me." Mom groans as she rubs her leg. "A bullet couldn't have hurt much worse."

"Except you'd be in the hospital or dead!" Gran Nola's voice rises with anger. "Katherine, your job is dangerous! Did you have that violent kid arrested?"

"I couldn't do that." Mom shakes her head. "I felt terrible for taking the little girl's dog. Besides, she's only four."

Gran Nola scowls. "What was a four-year-old doing with a paintball gun?"

"Apparently, the whole family plays paintball." Mom winces and sinks further into the recliner. "I just want to rest for a few minutes, then take the longest, hottest shower of my life."

"Of course, honey." Gran Nola's tone immediately softens. "I'm so sorry you had to go through this. I'll heat you up some peppermint tea."

As Gran Nola heads for the kitchen, Leo comes out carrying the puppy. He places her in my arms, then whispers, "Did you tell your mom about Buggy yet?"

"No." I tighten my grip on the wiggly puppy. "Not a good time."

Mom's eyes are closed, and I start to tiptoe away from the recliner so I don't disturb her. But Buggy has other ideas. She leaps out of my arms and plops on Mom's lap.

With a startled scream, my mother bolts up in the chair.

"Sorry, Mom," I say quickly. "I didn't mean for her to jump on you."

The tiny dog licks her arm, and Mom's expression softens. "Whose pup is this?"

"We don't know," I say. "We hoped you'd help us find out." I quickly explain how Major led us to the deserted barn and came out carrying a mouthful of puppy.

"We named her Buggy," Becca adds with a sweet smile.

Mom's eyes sharpen as she studies the puppy. "She's too young to be away from her mother. Did you talk to the neighbors where you found her?"

"There weren't any houses, just fields and the old barn," I say. "I didn't see a street sign, but it's on a dirt road off Grove Street."

"I think I know the place," Mom says with a thoughtful expression. "Is there a locked gate with a no-trespassing sign and a barn that's falling down?"

"Yeah," I answer.

"And this pup was alone?"

I nod. "Until Major rescued her."

Leo pats the pup on her head. "It's a mystery how she got there."

"Mom, would you check for an ID chip with your magic wand?"

"Electronic, not magic. She's much too young for a chip, but it can't hurt to check. You know where I keep it in my work truck." Mom tosses me the keys to her truck. "Bring it to me, and I'll scan her."

Mom is sipping herbal tea when I return with the scanner. It's cream colored and about the size of a TV remote. Mom presses a button and waves the device over Buggy. A light flashes. "Negative," Mom says. "No chip. But there may be a lost-pet report tomorrow. I'll check in the morning." She returns Buggy to me, then sinks back into the recliner with an exhausted sigh.

I whisper to my friends. "Mom needs to rest. Want to hang out in my room?"

"I can't stay," Leo says, taking his gyro-board controller from his pocket. "I have to go home for dinner."

"Me too." Becca holds out her arms for the puppy, and I kiss Buggy's soft head before handing her over. "I already texted Mom so she knows I'm bringing her home. Call me if your mother finds out anything."

"I will," I promise, waving as my friends leave.

After a quick dinner of leftover lasagna, I do my homework at the dining table so I don't wake Mom. When I start to yawn, I hug my grandmother good night and tiptoe into the guest room. There's a faint scent of Mom's tangerine shampoo, and the room is dark except for silvery moonlight slanting through the curtains. Mom is already in the king-size bed we share, curled beneath the handmade quilt—a gift from one of Gran Nola's yoga students.

My eyes adjust quickly to the dark. I have great night vision, a useful trait for a spy. Still, I almost trip over something—a shoe?—as I go to my dresser, open the second drawer, and feel for my pajamas. I put them on and slip under the covers. As I do, Mom stirs.

"Sorry," I say quietly. "I didn't mean to wake you."

"It's okay. I couldn't sleep anyway."

"Your leg hurting?"

"That and other things." Sighing, she pulls the quilt up to her chin. "I have a lot on my mind."

"Thinking about Dad?" I ask softly.

"Always," she admits. "I miss him."

There's something cozy and safe about the darkness, blurring our roles of mother and daughter so it's more like we're friends sharing confidences at a sleepover. "Mom, can I ask you something?"

"Sure, Kelsey."

"If you miss Dad, why didn't you stay with him?"

"Things have been tense since we lost the cottage. I didn't want to stay at the castle, but your father did."

Her bitter tone startles me, and I shift on my side to face her. "But Bragg Castle is amazing. Your suite is gorgeous with a huge TV and a jacuzzi. No cooking, cleaning, or doing laundry."

"I didn't notice you offering to stay there," she says wryly.

"I would have if Mr. Bragg allowed pets." I glance over at Honey curled in her kitty bed. "But you could have stayed and lived in luxury like a princess."

"Luxury is overrated." Mom blows out a sigh. "And I need to relax after I get home from a hard day at work."

"Catching stray animals doesn't seem that hard," I say.

"I do much more than that." She laughs wryly. "There's a reason I'm called an officer. While most of my calls are routine, like barking complaints and loose dogs, I deal with criminal activity too. Last month I worked with the sheriff to shut down a puppy mill and a dogfighting ring. It breaks my heart when animals are abused. But when I'm at the castle, I'm expected to smile and can't talk to your father about things…well, some things we need to work out. And there's zero privacy." She sighs. "Once I came out of my shower wearing only a towel to find the housekeeper, Sergei, folding my underwear."

"Oh no! How embarrassing!"

"For both of us. Poor man blushes now whenever he sees me." Mom rolls onto her back and stares up at the ceiling. "Your father thought it was funny. Being the chef for a famous man has gone to his head. I called him earlier today for advice on a difficult work situation, but he wouldn't take me seriously."

"What situation?" I sit up in bed.

"A call I went on yesterday bothered me. I didn't find anything suspicious, but now there's new information." She pauses. "It's probably nothing, but I'm going to check it out in the morning."

Something in her tone makes me nervous, and I remember how scared I was when I thought she was bleeding. "Mom, don't do anything risky."

"I won't. If I find proof of a crime, I'll report it to Sheriff Fischer and he'll take over. There's nothing to worry about."

"But I am worried," I confess. "Not just about your job…about you and Dad. You seem mad at him. Why did you really leave the castle?"

There's a long pause. "Your father and I need some time apart…to figure things out. The constant moving and lack of stability has been hard on our relationship."

My heart plummets. "Are you getting a divorce?"

"Of course not. We're just taking a break. Your father and I will be fine." She reaches across the blankets to squeeze my hand. "I miss him. So tomorrow morning I'm going to call him. We'll work things out, and I may even move back into the castle."

"I'm glad." I pause, wanting to be honest. "But I'm kind of sad too. I mean, it's been nice with just the two of us talking like…well…friends. This doesn't happen much."

"I'll make sure it happens more often. I get busy sometimes, but I'm always here for you, sweetie, and I want to know what's going on with you." Mom playfully tugs on my hair. "I can't believe your school year is almost over. Are there any seventh-grade parties or activities?"

"Well…there is a dance. But I'm not going," I add quickly.

"Isn't there a boy you like? Be bold and brave, and ask him to the dance."

"Leo asked me as a friend...not as a date." I'm glad she can't see my burning cheeks. "But I don't have anything to wear."

"I'm sure your sisters will loan you a pretty dress."

I press my lips together. *Hand-me-down Kelsey.* Never anything new, only secondhand castoffs from my sisters.

"If you haven't noticed, I'm shorter than Kiana and Kenya. It doesn't matter anyway because I'm going to tell Leo I can't go."

"What if I took you shopping?" Mom's voice wraps around me like a warm hug. "Would you go if you had a fantastic new dress?"

"Uh...maybe. But I'd need fantastic new shoes too."

"All right, a dress and shoes." I can't clearly see Mom's face, but her voice is smiling. "We'll make it a lunch date, and you can choose where to go. How does that sound?"

"Great! Can we go this weekend?"

"Your father and I will be house hunting. How about the following weekend?"

"The dance is next Friday." I frown.

She's quiet for a moment. "Then we'll go tomorrow afternoon. I'll call the school and arrange for you to leave early. Be sure to get your assignments from your teachers. I'll take off early from work and pick you up at noon."

"You won't get too busy?" I ask.

"I'll be there. I promise." She leans in to kiss my cheek. "There's no way I'd miss taking my beautiful youngest daughter shopping for her first school dance."

At noon the next day, I stand outside the school.

I wait and wait and wait for Mom.

But she never comes.

- Chapter 4 -
Missing Mom

Eventually, Dad comes to get me. He drives up, rolling down the window. "Hop in, Kelsey."

I dump my backpack in the backseat and fasten my seat belt. My stomach is knotted so tightly that I'm sure I can't speak. I want to explode with anger. When I finally gave up on waiting for Mom and went to the school office to call her, I got her voice mail. *Leave a message after the beep*. Well, you can bet I left a message. One she will *never* forget.

"Kelsey, what's going on?" Dad asks as he pulls out of the school parking lot. "You didn't make much sense when you called. Why didn't your mother pick you up?"

"She forgot me." I stare out the window, anger morphing into hurt.

"She must have gotten busy at work. Again," Dad says, not in defense but with bitterness that matches my own feelings. "I don't understand what's going on with her. If I could just talk to her…"

I turn from the window to stare at Dad. "Didn't she call you?"

"No." He slows for a red light, glancing at me with a guarded expression. "Why? Was she going to?"

I nod. "She said she'd call you this morning."

"Well, she didn't. And when I tried to call her, it went to voice mail." Dad taps his fingers on the steering wheel like he's impatient for the light to turn green. He glances at me curiously. "Why are you out of school early? Do you have a doctor's appointment?"

"No appointment…Mom and I planned to do some shopping."

He scowls. "She has time to shop but not to return my call?"

Dad slows the car to the speed limit, then looks sheepishly over at me. "Sorry, Kelsey. It's your mother I'm mad at. Not you."

"I'm not happy with her myself," I admit. "But

she might have a good excuse…an emergency at work, or maybe her truck broke down."

As I'm saying this, Dad's cell phone dings. Since he's driving, I grab his phone. "A text from"—I glance down and my heart leaps—"Mom."

"About time," Dad says sharply, but there's relief in his tone. He asks me to read the text out loud.

Leaving for few days.

Need time alone.

Don't call.

It's Mom's familiar phone number and icon with her smiling face—but there's no smiling in the words. I reel with hurt. Last night when Mom and I talked, I felt really close to her, pleased that she was confiding in me. But she didn't say anything about leaving.

Did I only imagine our closeness?

I feel even worse for Dad. He calls her back but gets her voice mail and retreats into a silence that has weight and substance like thunderclouds. I was so sure Mom would work things out with Dad and they'd find us a great new house so our family would be together again.

He doesn't say anything as he drives me to my grandmother's house, only a curt *bye* as the door bangs shut behind me.

Gran Nola is busy with a client in the exercise room. I hear her instructing *Lift your leg*, *Hold that stretch*, and *Reach higher* as I stomp into my bedroom. I drop my backpack on the floor. Inside are pages of homework—the assignments I collected from my teachers since I left early. What a waste of time. I should have stayed at school for lunch and my last classes. I even canceled my plans for a CCSC meeting with Leo and Becca after school. Instead of hanging out with my friends at the Skunk Shack, I stood on a curb waiting alone.

Scooping up Honey, I curl up on my bed and stare out the window at an endless gray sky.

How could Mom forget me?

My gaze sweeps around the room. Mom's running shoes rest on her black leather suitcase where she kicked them off. Her makeup case, brush, and wire-rimmed reading glasses are on her nightstand. And the faint scent of her shampoo lingers on the air like the ghost of Mom is still in the room.

She promised, I think, as a tear slides down my cheek and onto Honey's thick orange fur. Holding Honey close to my heart, I'm comforted by her rumbling purr. Hurt shifts into anger, and I come to a decision. Mom may have ruined our plans, but I won't let her ruin my day.

Leaving Honey on the bed, I go into the living room where Gran Nola usually has her phone charging. As the youngest in a large family, I don't have my own cell phone. So I borrow Gran's phone to text Becca and Leo:

Meeting on.

C U @ SS

Biking along the bumpy trail to the Skunk Shack always feels like I'm traveling deep into the woods. But our clubhouse is only a short uphill walk from Becca's home at Wild Oaks Animal Sanctuary.

It was Becca's idea to turn the old shack into the CCSC clubhouse. Cleaning it was a challenge because birds and other wild creatures had nested there for years. But after lots of scrubbing and sweeping, and after we painted the walls a sunny shade of yellow, our clubhouse now looks great. We keep a few pieces of furniture we found there: a stained table, chairs, a cabinet for storing supplies, and an antique grandfather clock that

Leo repaired. Now the clock chimes musically every hour.

Becca's bike isn't propped against the table-sized stump, but Leo's gyro-board leans near the clubhouse door. When I step inside, I find Leo sitting at the table, staring down at something metallic in his hands. This is the first time Leo and I have been alone since the robot convention, and I smooth back a loose strand of my hair, hoping he doesn't ask about the dance.

"Where's Becca?" I try to sound normal.

Leo doesn't look up. "I assume she's on her way here."

"What's that?" I peer over his shoulder. Wires twist down into opposite sides of a pen-like device. He creates cool inventions like the dragon drone, a tiny dragonfly drone that flies high for covert spy missions. And his key spider—a metal circle of adjustable keys—can pick almost any lock.

"A poly-truth pen." Leo proudly lifts the gadget. "When it's finished, it'll assess three indicators of lying: respiration, heart rate, and skin conductivity."

Curious, I lean in for a closer look. "Like a lie detector?"

"That's my objective. I wanted to show it to you at lunch today, but you left school early. Becca said you had an appointment with your mother."

"I did." I sink into my lopsided chair at the table. Before I can explain what happened, I hear the familiar braking of Becca's bike.

Becca rushes in, out of breath like she pedaled at superspeed. She wipes sweat from her brow and pushes away a loose strand of pink-streaked hair. Even sweaty, she looks cute and stylish in black jeans with leopard-patterned pockets and a zebra-striped jacket over a silky white blouse.

"Sorry I'm late." Becca plops into her chair. "I was teaching Buggy to eat puppy food. She's stubborn...but I'm stubborner, so she finally ate."

"*Stubborner* is not a word," Leo says.

"Well, it should be." Becca flashes a wide grin. "Totally fits me when I'm working with animals."

"I can't wait to see Buggy again," I say. "I was hoping you'd bring her."

"She's sleeping, but come over after our meeting and you can cuddle her. She's so sweet. If I didn't already have a zillion animals, I'd keep her. Mom is positive she's a purebred pug and thinks she must have wandered away from her owners. Did your mother show you the newest missing-dog reports?"

"No." Anger rises hot to my cheeks. "She didn't pick me up from school."

"Seriously?" Becca flips her ponytail over her shoulder.

Leo frowns. "What happened?"

"Mom forgot me. I waited and waited, only she didn't come," I say, my throat tight. "Since I don't have my own phone, I had to go into the school office to call her. But all I got was her voice mail. Finally, I called Dad."

"Oh no!" Becca's hand flies to her mouth. "She'd never just forget you without a good reason. Did something happen to her?"

"I worried about that, but then she texted Dad. She told him she needs time alone so she's leaving for a few days." She didn't even mention me, I think, my eyes welling up.

"Your mother left?" Becca asks in disbelief.

Leo wrinkles his brow. "Where did she go?"

"I have no idea. Somewhere far away from us, I guess," I add bitterly. "She told Dad not to call her."

Becca's forehead creases. "But when we talked at school, you said your mother was going to work things out with your father and move back to the castle."

"That's what she told me. She also promised to pick me up from school. She lied."

"Parents don't always behave like adults," Leo says. "Before my parents separated, they argued like my house was a war zone. But now they get along great."

"My parents are *not* separating," I say through clenched teeth.

"Of course they aren't." Becca reaches over to squeeze my hand.

"We were going to have a special day, just the two of us..." My throat tightens. "But I guess it didn't matter to her."

"Or something happened to her." Leo stares off toward the shuttered window, tapping his poly-truth pen on the table like each tap is a thought bubble ready to pop. "Are you sure the text was from your mother?"

I nod, then repeat what the text said, cringing at the *I need time alone* part.

"Has she ever done anything like this before?" Leo asks.

"No." I swallow a bitter lump of hurt. "She's

always on time or early."

Becca frowns. "What if she hit her head and lost her memory?"

"Highly improbable," Leo says. "Amnesia is more common in fiction than in reality."

"Kelsey, you need to talk to your mom to find out what's going on." Becca takes her phone from her pocket. "Call her."

"I've already tried that."

Becca holds out her phone. "Try again."

I press my lips tightly as I tap in the number. I'm torn between wanting to scream at Mom and wanting to make sure she's all right. When the rings change to voice mail, I toss the phone back to Becca.

"Clearly she does *not* want to talk to me," I say angrily.

"She could be in an area without cellular signal, or maybe she mislaid her phone," Leo suggests. "My mother used to lose hers until I attached a tracking app."

"Mom never leaves without her phone, but apparently she's fine with leaving her family."

"It just doesn't make sense." Becca purses her peach-frosted lips. "I don't believe she'd go away."

I remember Mom's paint-splattered uniform. She hadn't been seriously hurt, but if an angry child could shoot her, what would an angry adult do? When Mom started working as an animal control officer and explained that the sheriff was her boss, I thought this was weird. I didn't think that protecting animals was dangerous like catching criminals. But what if it is?

A sudden thought makes me gasp.

"Mom's suitcase was still in our room *after* she sent the text. Why would she go away without her suitcase?" My words trail off in fear.

I think of other things Mom left behind: shoes, makeup, and even her reading glasses.

She would never leave me waiting at the school or break a promise.

What really happened to my mother?

Chapter 5

Suspicions

I jump from my chair. "I have to call the sheriff!"

"No need to call him," Becca says. "He's at my house. Mom invited Sheriff Fischer over for dinner. When I left, he was just driving in."

Fears for my mother whirl as we hop on our wheels and race down the trail to the wild animal sanctuary.

Fenced animal enclosures, outbuildings, and a barn blur by. I pedal so fast that I'm the first to reach Becca's L-shaped ranch style home. It's a huge relief to see the sheriff's official car parked in the driveway. He'll know what to do. He'll find Mom and bring her home safely.

Becca and Leo are close behind me as I burst into the house. In the kitchen, Becca's mother is handing a steaming coffee cup to the sheriff. Sheriff Fischer is a stocky man with dark hair and a rugged, tanned face. Instead of a uniform with a shiny badge and holster, he's wearing dark-navy pants and a light-blue shirt.

Mrs. Morales turns to look at me, her quick smile fading to alarm when I rush past her to the sheriff. "Mom's in trouble!"

He sets down his coffee cup on the table. "What's happened?" He glances around. "Where is she?"

I shake my head. "I don't know."

"Tell me what you do know," he says.

"Mom's missing! No time to explain! Put out an AMBER Alert or something to find her!"

"Calm down, Kelsey," he says. "I can't do anything until I have the facts."

Becca slips her arm around me. "Go ahead, Kelsey. Tell him everything."

"Mom promised to pick me up at school. I waited and waited for like an hour, but she never came." I speak so quickly that my words tumble over themselves. "So I called Dad to come get me and he hadn't heard from Mom either, but then he got a text from her saying she was leaving for a few days. Only Mom would never leave without telling us."

Mrs. Morales and the sheriff exchange a look, and I can tell they don't believe me.

"But she did tell your father...in that text," Sheriff Fischer points out. "Kelsey, I understand you're upset, but I doubt your mother is in any danger. Have you tried calling her back?"

"Of course I did! But it goes to her voice mail. If she was busy at work, she would have asked Dad or my grandmother to pick me up. But she didn't call anyone and just left me waiting."

Becca's mother comes over to put her arm around me. "Kelsey, I'm sure she's fine."

"But she wouldn't just leave like that!" My voice sharpens with frustration. "She didn't even take her suitcase!"

Sheriff Fischer's dark brows slant together. "She left her suitcase?"

I nod, biting my lip as fears rise.

"Did she take any of her belongings?"

"I don't know, but she left stuff that she usually takes with her." I think back to my bedroom. "Sneakers, brush, makeup, and reading glasses."

"Hmm" is all he says as he sits down at the table

and stirs a spoon in his coffee cup, thinking. After a moment, he sets the spoon aside and reaches for his phone. He taps a few buttons, and his volume is set so loud I can hear ringing. Then a cheerful woman's voice says, "Sun Flower Animal Control."

"Hey, Michelle," the sheriff says briskly. "Have you seen Katherine today?"

I hold my breath, afraid of what I might find out.

"Is that so?" His casual tone gives nothing away, and I can only hear a faint murmur from Michelle. "What time was this?...Uh-huh...Uh-huh..." He mutters a few more "uh-huhs," then says thanks and hangs up.

I suck in a scared breath. "What did you find out?"

He pulls out a chair from the table and gestures for me to sit beside him. "Kelsey, your mother reported to work as usual this morning."

I nod, not surprised since I'd watched her put on her uniform and leave.

"But when she came in, she arranged for another officer, Lamar Jefferson, to take over her shift. She told Michelle she needed the day off for personal reasons."

"She didn't work at all?" My mouth falls open.

"But she was only planning to take the afternoon off."

"You'll have to ask her about that. Until then, you can stop worrying because wherever she went was her idea." He drums his fingers on the table and clears his throat. "Kelsey, I'm aware there are problems between your parents, and I'm sorry. But as her boss, I can't get involved in family matters."

"It's not a family matter! She's missing because of her job." I push the chair back and stand. "Last night, Mom told me she was suspicious about a call she investigated on Wednesday."

He arches one dark brow. "Which one?"

"I don't know. She told me she found new information and planned to check it out today. She said if her suspicions were right, she'd tell you."

"She didn't mention it to me."

"So she must have gone alone. If she did, she could have been attacked and..." I shudder, afraid to imagine the worst.

"But I already told you that she didn't work today," he says with a weary sigh. "Lamar took her shift."

"Then why did she wear her uniform when she left this morning?"

"She probably wasn't sure someone could take over for her." He shrugs. "I don't know exactly what went down. I'm sure she'll tell you when she gets home."

"*If* she does," I say with a desperate sense of time running out. "She was already attacked once this week."

"Kelsey, is that what this is about?" The sheriff's expression softens, and he pats my hand. "Are you worried because of the paintball incident?"

"No." I shake my head. "Although it proved her job could be dangerous."

"While being an animal control officer can be challenging, there's seldom any danger—except from an angry four-year-old." His mouth twitches like he's trying not to smile.

"But what if something bad *did* happen?" I argue.

"Here's my advice to you. Your mother wants some time alone, so give it to her."

Becca's mother slips her arm over my shoulder. "Honey, why don't you stay here for dinner?"

"I don't want dinner. I want my mother back," I say stubbornly.

The adults share uneasy glances, and I can tell they think I'm overreacting.

"Kelsey, sometimes marriages need a break," Mrs. Morales adds with a sweet smile identical to Becca's. "This is between your parents and has nothing to do with you. Your mother will contact you when she's ready."

I blink fast, pushing back the tears. I think back to this morning when I last saw Mom. I was waking up, and she was already dressed in her uniform. She bent over and kissed my check, whispering good-bye. Was that good-bye more final than I realized? If she was planning to leave, why didn't she tell me? Why promise to take me shopping, then leave me waiting at school?

Leo is watching me, frowning as if he doesn't know what to say.

Becca reaches out for my hand. "Want to go see Buggy?" When I don't move, she tugs me down the hall. "Come on."

I follow numbly. All I can think about is my mother. Could I be wrong about Mom? Is she enjoying "time alone" in a comfortable hotel? Did she simply forget to pick me up?

Buggy is in a crate with blankets, toys, food, and water. When Becca lifts her, Buggy wiggles excitedly, yapping. She looks much better than she did yesterday. Her tummy is full, and her black eyes shine brightly. Becca, Leo, and I take turns cuddling her until Becca returns her to the crate, where she promptly falls asleep. Then we go into Becca's upside-down room.

There is no carpet or rugs, and her belongings are arranged overhead on the walls, out of the reach of animals. A bookshelf with Becca's favorite animal books winds around the edge of the ceiling. And the ceiling decor includes a cork bulletin board, nature paintings, and dangling county-fair award ribbons. A rolling ladder propped against the wall gives Becca quick access to her belongings and lets her reach high enough that so cats, dogs, and goats won't get into her things.

The only animal in her room is Chris, one of the three kittens we rescued. The black cat is curled between pillows on the queen-size bed. When I sit beside her, Chris crawls into my lap.

Leo gives me a worried look. "Kelsey, are you okay?"

"I don't know. Am I freaking out over nothing?" I run my fingers through Chris's silky fur. "Maybe Sheriff Fischer is right and Mom left because she wants to be alone—like the text said."

"Analyze the facts," Leo says with typical Leo logic. He takes out his mini-tablet and taps on the screen. "Fact one: Your mother admitted that she and your father were taking a break from each other. Fact two: She went to work this morning but then took the day off. Fact three: She sent a text to your father saying she was leaving."

"Which is a good thing," Becca says with forced optimism, "because if she can send a text, then she's safe."

"I guess so." Hurt feelings ache like a deep bruise. "The facts prove Mom left town to get away from her family and isn't in danger."

"Au contraire." Leo waves his hand. "There are additional facts to consider. Fact four: Not picking you up from school is out of character. Fact five: Your mother told you she was suspicious about a work call. Fact six: She neglected to take her suitcase. Does she have another suitcase?"

"Yes, but it's in storage with our furniture."

Leo nods. "According to my calculations, there are two probable explanations. One: your mother doesn't want to be found. Two: an unknown person doesn't want her to be found."

A chill sweeps through me.

Becca and Leo look at me like they're waiting for a plan of action. I study spy novels and put the word Spy in the Curious Cat Spy Club. I'm good at solving puzzling mysteries about abused or abandoned animals, but this is about my mother. What can I do?

"I need proof that Mom investigated a suspicious call so that Sheriff Fischer will search for her," I say. "But I don't know what type of call it was or where it came from."

"How many calls does she go on each day?" Becca asks.

"A few dozen?" I shrug. "I have no idea."

Leo taps his finger to his chin. "Today is Friday. Your mother went out on the suspicious call two days ago."

"Yeah, on Wednesday. But the sheriff wouldn't even check her daily log to find out where she went." I press my lips together to hold back my anger.

"We'll find her ourselves." Leo stands up from the chair, his blue eyes shining with determination. "And I know where to start."

- Chapter 6 -
Z Codes

When I get home, I rush into the kitchen where Gran Nola is tossing a salad and shout, "Mom is missing!"

Instead of being shocked, my grandmother calmly shows me a text she received from Mom. It's the same text I read on Dad's phone.

"I've already talked to your father, so I know what's going on. Your mother needs time alone to think things through." Gran Nola picks up a knife and slices a tomato. "Don't worry."

"But she didn't pick me up from school!"

"Your father told me about that. I'm really disappointed in her," my grandmother says as she chops the tomato into tiny pieces. "She should have asked me or your father to pick you up."

"But she didn't even pack a suitcase! All of her things are still in the guest room."

"Not all of them." Gran Nola dumps the tomato slices into a bowl. "She keeps an overnight bag in her truck in case she needs a change of clothes."

My mouth falls open. "I didn't know that."

"I wish Katherine would have talked to me or your father instead of running away. But she's been so stressed lately that a long weekend alone will be good for her." My grandmother pats my hand. "She'll feel better when she comes back."

If she comes back, I think with a stab of fear.

But there's no point in trying to convince my grandmother that Mom is in danger. Just like Dad and the sheriff and Mrs. Morales, she believes the texts more than I do.

Fortunately, my club mates believe me. As I'm getting ready for bed that evening, Leo calls. "Come to my house at 8:00 a.m. tomorrow for a CCSC meeting. I have something important to show you," he adds mysteriously before hanging up.

What does he want to show me? I hope that it's something that leads to my mother. Without her, my room echoes with emptiness. Mom's sneakers are still on her suitcase where she kicked them off. When I check her dresser drawers and the closet, nothing seems to be missing—except the work uniform she was wearing. And her green toothbrush is still in the bathroom.

No matter what the adults think, I know Mom did not *plan* to leave.

I sleep restlessly and wake up before my alarm goes off. A glance at my clock brings all my fears back. I've heard the first twenty-four hours are the most critical to finding a missing person. Mom has been gone for longer than that, and no one thinks she's missing—except the CCSC.

When I arrive at Leo's house, Becca's already there, wearing black tights, a panther-black shirt, and a knit black beanie. She's staring up at the ceiling, aiming a remote control at Leo's micro-sized dragonfly drone, which circles over her head. The robotic dragonfly camera eyes transmit images so I can see a ceiling view of Leo's room on a monitor. The room is more like a high-tech office than a bedroom, with computers, robots, and floor-to-ceiling shelves stacked with containers of electronic parts. And humming with bubbling sounds is a large aquarium with exotic fish named after characters in *Finding Nemo*. Leo the tech genius has a secret love of Disney movies.

Leo gestures for me to sit beside him. He spins his wheeled desk chair back to the computer and clicks on the keyboard at superspeed. Numbers and symbols swirl across the screen so fast it makes me dizzy.

Becca maneuvers the drone as it loops around the ceiling. She glances at me with a hopeful look. "Any news?"

"Yeah, but nothing good." I bite my lip. "Dad's not the only one who got a text from Mom. My grandmother, sisters, and brother did too. And they all got the exact same text."

"You probably would have gotten one too, if you had a cell phone," Becca says sympathetically. She knows how much I long for my own phone.

"If I'd gotten the text, I wouldn't have believed it." I fold my arms across my chest. "But my family does, and they think I'm freaking out over nothing."

"Even though no one knows where your mom is?" Becca jerks the remote as she turns to look at me, almost crashing the metal dragonfly into a shelf.

"Everyone thinks Mom took a long weekend away and will return by tomorrow. Gran Nola said she's done this before, but I don't remember Mom ever leaving like this. No one else is worried."

"We'll find her," Leo says in such a confident tone that my heart warms.

"Leo has a plan," Becca adds. She lowers the drone to the floor, then shuts off the remote.

"I found the key to your mother's location." Leo taps rapidly on a keyboard. Lights flash on a nearby printer, and it pushes out a sheet of paper that Leo hands to me.

At the top of the page are the silhouettes of a cat and a dog framing the logo: Animal Control Officer Call Log. I try to make sense of a chart with columns labeled Time Rec'd, Time Resp., Time Clear, Call #, Address, Type, and Action. And at the bottom of the page is my mother's name.

"Mom's call log," I say with a rush of excitement.

Leo flashes a proud grin. "For Wednesday."

"How did you get this? Did you hack into Mom's email?"

"Hacking is a crude term and unnecessary in this situation. The Animal Control Department is a public service, and therefore call records are accessible to the public—if you know where to look." Leo flashes a sly grin. "The public records for last week are currently available, but this week hasn't been posted. So I bypassed a few obstacles to find the log for Wednesday."

Time Rec'd	Time Resp.	Address	Type
8:27 AM	8:45 AM	2575 Duncan Street	ZMISC
9:54 AM	10:12 AM	34 Blackberry Lane	ZDTHF
11:01 AM	11:26 AM	1933 Larkspur Lane	ZWELF
11:43 AM	12:01 PM	17 Vine Road	ZABAND
12:15 PM	12:45 PM	30 Nogard Drive	ZVIC
2:11 PM	2:19 PM	116 Pearl Street	ZATTAK
3:35 PM	3:52 PM	56 Titian Court	ZBITE
4:04 PM	4:17 PM	38 Applewood Drive	ZINJ

He hands me the paper, and I study the entries. The first three columns show the times for each call Mom went on from 8:27 a.m. to 4:04 p.m. I recognize most of the street names since I've ridden my bike all over Sun Flower searching for lost pets. The last column (Action) lists letters that make no sense to me. ZVIC, ZINJ, and ZWELF don't look like any code I've seen in my *Decoding Codes* book.

"What do all the numbers and letters mean?" I ask Leo.

"Times, locations, type of calls," Leo replies. "It's easy to read."

For a genius like him. Confused, I point to the column with letters beginning with Z. "What is ZVIC?"

"Vicious animal."

"Oh, I get it," I say. "Ignore the Z and the VIC is short for *vicious*."

"Precisely," Leo says as if this is as obvious as adding two plus two. "Z is probably an official code representing the Animal Control Department."

"ZWELF sounds like elf." I wrinkle my brow. "What does it mean?"

"WELF is an abbreviation for welfare."

"Animal welfare." Becca's half-moon necklace dangles as she bends over for a closer look at the paper. "Someone reported an abused or neglected animal."

Leo nods. "When the sheriff's office gets a report about animals, they send an animal control officer to investigate."

"Like my mom," I say with a sick feeling in my gut.

The paper rustles in Leo's hand. "Each code represents one of the calls your mother investigated. The Z codes are easy to interpret once you ignore the Z. ZINJ means an injured animal, ZATTAK an animal attack, and ZABAND is for an abandoned dog."

I run my finger down the coded column.

"Mom went on eight calls on Wednesday," I say as I count down the list in Leo's hands. "The next day she found out something suspicious about one of them, so she was going to go back Friday morning. We have to find her."

"We will," Leo says with a determined set to his jaw. "Even if it means going to each address on this list."

"And doing what?" Becca spreads her arms out. "We can't just knock on doors and ask, 'Did you kidnap Kelsey's mother?'"

"Subtle methods are required," Leo agrees with a thoughtful expression. "I'll do more research online. But don't worry. We'll find your mother."

His confidence is so reassuring that I want to hug him. Of course, I don't...and I blush a little at the thought.

"I'll print out directions to each address," Leo

says, turning back to his computer. "Then we'll start our search at the closest location."

"No, we need to start where Mom did." I lean over Leo's shoulder to skim down the list of addresses. I recognize most of the streets, which spread in every direction across Sun Flower. "My spy books say if you're tracking someone you have to become them."

"How do we become your mother?" Becca purses her peach-frosted lips. "We're just middle schoolers."

"If we shadow Mom's trail from her first work call to the last, we're more likely to discover which call made her suspicious." When I realize I'm touching Leo's arm, I quickly pull back.

Leo's gaze meets mine. "Good suggestion."

"Um, thanks." My cheeks warm. "What's the first address?"

Leo pulls up a map of Sun Flower on his screen, then prints it out. He scrawls eight circles on the page with a red marker and labels them one through eight. "At 8:45 a.m., your mother went to 2575 Duncan Street for a ZMISC report." He points to the red circled one.

"What's ZMISC?" I peer at the paper.

"A miscellaneous report," Leo answers. "That indicates the report didn't match the usual complaints."

"Which tells us nothing." Becca throws up her hands. "Miscellaneous might as well be 7-UNKNOWN."

"And it could be risky." I frown, remembering saying this to my mother.

Suddenly I'm afraid, not just for Mom but for Becca and Leo too.

Am I leading my friends into danger?

- Chapter 7 -
Duncan Street

Leo packs his leather pouch with his bird drone, dragon drone, and FRODO.

The 4.0 version of the bird drone looks like a metal bird and can fly far and high for aerial surveillance. The dragon drone is a silver-winged dragonfly robot that's tinier than a thumb with metallic glassy eyes and translucent wings. The bug-like eyes are actually cameras that videotape images. And the largest drone is FRODO (aka Futuristic Robotic Odor Detection Operative). It's a metal dish with dozens of tiny wheels on the bottom and weird black bumps covering the top that are powerful smell receptors made of frog eggs. FRODO can track odors like a search-and-sniff rescue robot.

Becca and Leo head for Duncan Street, but since FRODO needs something with Mom's scent to track, I detour to my grandmother's house.

I rush into the guest room and search through my mother's dresser drawers, sniffing shirts, pants, and socks for something that smells like Mom. But everything is neatly folded and smells of lavender-scented fabric softener. I even check the hamper, hoping for sweaty workout clothes—but it's empty. *Drats.*

Sighing, I turn from the hamper, and my gaze falls on Mom's white sneakers with green laces that she left on her suitcase. They haven't been washed in a while and are smudged with grass and dirt stains. Mom loves these shoes and wears them when she gardens. I only need one shoe and choose the dirtiest one.

Since Leo is bringing his spy robots, I'll bring my spy pack. I climb on a stool to reach the high shelf where I hid my green spy pack. It's an ordinary green backpack filled with extraordinary spy tools like graphite powder, gloves, a flash cap, a laser pointer, night vision glasses, and disguises.

Zipping open the backpack, I push aside a magnifying glass and duct tape. I find the box of plastic "evidence" bags and slip Mom's shoe inside one of them. Slinging the bulky pack over my shoulders, I race outside, hop on my bike, and ride off to join my friends.

Winding through Sun Flower reminds me of previous CCSC cases. A zorse named Zed ran into traffic on Pleasant Street, which led us to the alley where Becca, Leo, and I rescued three kittens from a dumpster. A few more turns, and I pass a familiar yard full of golden sunflowers where Sunflower Mary, a crafty old woman, rocks in her porch chair, yellow crochet yarn dangling down her skirt. A few streets later, I see the spiraling turret of the Victorian-styled home where the CCSC first met Albert, a 130-year-old tortoise. Last week I got an email with a photo of Albert and his owner, Reggie. The tortoise looked happy as Reggie fed him a gigantic chunk of cactus.

The first address on Mom's call log is 2575 Duncan Street, a run-down apartment complex in the oldest part of downtown. I roll across uneven pavement stained with oil and skid marks, scanning the area for my club mates. Rows of cars are crowded in the parking lot, but no one seems to be around. Where are Becca and Leo?

I circle, wondering if I got the address wrong—until I spy a blond head crouched behind a laundromat.

I park my bike next to Becca's, and Leo stops tinkering with FRODO to look up at me. "Did you bring an odoriferous object?"

"If you mean something that smells like Mom, yes. Here's her shoe." I take the bagged shoe from my spy pack.

"I love colorful laces." Becca playfully swats at the dangling green shoelace. "I have purple, blue, and pink laces so my sneakers match my clothes."

"Mom only has green. It's her favorite color." I sigh as I hand the shoe over to Leo. "So which apartment are we going to?"

"The apartment number is…" Leo frowns at the call log. "Not listed."

"Seriously?" Becca arches her dark brows.

"So what do we do now?" I spread my arms in frustration. "We can't check *every* apartment. There must be hundreds."

"According to my calculations, there are seventy-five." Leo tilts his head thoughtfully. "Allowing five minutes for each location equals 375 minutes, so it would take six hours and fifteen minutes to investigate."

I frown up at the sprawling apartments. "That's too long."

"We won't have to check every apartment." Leo gestures to his leather pouch. "We'll use my bird drone to identify which ones have outdoor patios where pets might be kept. That will narrow down our search."

A few minutes later, the bird drone is poised for takeoff. I peer through my mini binoculars, Leo aims a remote at the bird drone, and Becca is on alert as our lookout.

"Ready, set"—Leo aims the remote at the bird-shaped drone—"launch!"

With a buzzing of robotic wings, the bird drone soars into the sky and toward the apartments. If anyone glances out their window, they'll just see the gray blur of a bird, unaware they're being spied upon.

The first time we used a bird drone, it worked for a while, then crashed. Fortunately, this is an improved model. As the drone moves from apartment to apartment, the tiny robot streams images to Leo's tablet.

"Doghouse sighted," Leo reports as he peers closely at his tablet.

I lean in to check out the screen, but the image is too small. Leo taps on the keyboard, enlarging the picture of a wooden, peaked dog house. The bird drone whirls on and more photos appear, showing us more evidence of pets: portable carriers, doghouses, water or food bowls, and carpeted cat trees for climbing.

"I have a confession," Leo says, his tone suddenly serious. "I was wrong about the number of apartments: not seventy-five, but seventy-six."

"Close enough." I smile because it's cute how he takes everything so seriously. "Even geniuses can make mistakes."

"It's a rare occurrence." Leo taps his remote, and the bird drone comes in for a landing. "Now we know that the apartments with animals are located in the left side. There are twenty pets: cats, dogs and a chicken pen."

"Chickens in an apartment?" I say, surprised.

"Raising chickens is popular because people love fresh eggs," Becca says. "But chickens can be noisy and probably are not allowed in the apartments."

"That might be the reason Mom came here." I snap my fingers. "A neighbor probably reported the chickens. Let's find out." I jump up, ready to storm the chicken apartment and ask about my mother.

Leo tucks the bird drone into his leather pouch and lifts out the platelike robot. "But your mother could have come here for a different reason, so I'll use FRODO to sniff out her scent. We'll position him near the apartments on the left."

"Can he climb stairs?" I ask with a glance at the steep staircase.

"No, but I'll carry him. His sensor lights will show me the right direction within a 35-foot perimeter, so I'll need to get closer to the apartments," Leo says. "Wait here. It's less conspicuous if I go alone."

As if a guy following a plate on wheels can be inconspicuous, I think with a half-smile.

Becca and I hide behind the laundromat while Leo places the sneaker on the ground. He flips a switch, and lights flash on FRODO's bubbly receptors. The robot rolls as slowly as a tortoise to the left...to the right...and spins completely around, rolling directly toward us.

"Why is it coming back?" I ask Leo.

"I don't know. Turn around, FRODO!" Leo frantically clicks remote buttons.

Becca's hands fly to her cheeks. "He's out of control!"

"And headed for me!" I jump back.

FRODO stops in front of my shoes—a light flashing from red to green like a spotlight aiming at me.

"Weird." I peer down. "What does the green light mean?"

"Target sighted. But you are *not* the target." Leo runs his fingers through his blond hair. "I don't understand why FRODO malfunctioned."

"Maybe he didn't," I say, a thought coming to me. "He followed Mom's scent—which led him to me. I may not be the target, but I held Mom's shoe and shared her room. To a super sniffer, I must smell like my mother."

Leo looks relieved as he nods. "Your mother's smell is three days old. Your smell is more potent."

"You think I stink?" I tease.

"No!" His cheeks redden. "What I meant was—"

"Yikes!" Becca points beyond us. "Look!"

I see the blue and red lights of a familiar official truck. "Uh-oh!" I groan. "The sheriff!"

"It's bad enough he's always hanging around my mother." Becca scowls as she crosses her arms over her chest. "Is he following me around?"

Sheriff Fischer strides over. "What are you kids doing here? I received a report of suspicious teens and find you three looking very suspicious."

"We were out for a ride," Becca tells him. This is the truth, just not all of it.

"Are you visiting someone who lives here?" He sweeps his hand toward the apartment building.

"Um...not exactly," I say, which sounds suspicious even to me.

Spy strategy 12: *Always be prepared with a cover story when on surveillance.*

"Kelsey, we've known each other for a while, and I hope you consider me a friend." Sheriff Fischer's tone softens. "Be honest with me. Is this about your mother?"

"Of course not. Why would you think that?"

"When I got the report from this address, I noticed that your mother responded to a call at this same address a few days ago." Sunlight flashes off his badge as he narrows his gaze at me. "It seems more than a coincidence to find you here."

I try to look innocent. "Mom was here?"

"I suspect you already know that."

"I don't know what you're talking about. But

since you said Mom was here, I'm curious why." I widen my eyes. "What was the report about?"

He studies me with a thoughtful expression. "I suppose it can't hurt to tell you. A resident panicked when he thought he saw a giant snake lurking in the bushes. But it turned out to be a garden hose. It was just a routine call and not at all dangerous. Don't get any ideas about playing Nancy Drew."

"Why would I do that when you've assured me my mother is fine?"

"Exactly." He crosses his arms over his chest. "So what are you kids doing here?"

"Um...we..." I falter.

"We're implementing a robotic experiment." Leo comes to my rescue like a knight in a shiny black vest. "It's a trial run for my futuristic robotic odor detection operative."

Sheriff Fischer knits his bushy brows. "A *what*?"

"My robot, sir." Leo gestures to the bubble-covered bot. "FRODO detects odors through olfactory receptors."

The sheriff leans in for a closer look. "I know a bit about robots since I was in a robotics club in college. But I've never heard of a robot that can smell."

"FRODO's olfactory system is programmed to recognize chemical signatures like blood and sweat," Leo explains proudly.

"Impressive." Sheriff Fischer lifts the brim of his cap to look closely at Leo. "You built this by yourself?"

"Of course he did." Becca rolls her eyes at the sheriff. "Leo's brilliant."

"He certainly is." Sheriff Fischer gives an appreciative whistle as he bends over to look at FRODO. "What's the energy source?"

"Solar strips," Leo says. "They're efficient and built into the casing."

"I built my robots from a kit. But yours is much more sophisticated. It's amazing what you've achieved here. How long have you been building robots?"

"Since I was four." Leo's voice warms with pride. "Well, three if you count the Lego bots."

"I wish I could let you stay, but the apartment manager wants you to leave." Sheriff Fischer frowns. "Sorry, but you'll have to find another place for your trial run."

Leo picks up FRODO. "We're done here anyway."

I nod because there's nothing suspicious about a

garden hose "snake." We might as well go on to the next address.

Sheriff Fischer pats Leo on the shoulder. "Next time you want to test a robot, there's an empty stretch of pavement behind the sheriff's office parking lot. Call me, and I'll clear it with my office."

"That's very kind of you, sir." Leo grins when the sheriff offers him a business card.

"See you kids later." Sheriff Fischer's keys jingle in his hands as he turns to Becca. "Actually, I'll see you tonight for dinner. I'm taking you and your mother out for Chinese food. How does that sound?"

Becca glances down at her purple glitter sneakers. "Great," she says with zero enthusiasm.

The sheriff opens his mouth like he wants to say something to her but then sighs and strides off to his truck.

"Becca, why were you rude to the sheriff?" Leo demands as he carefully tucks FRODO into his leather pouch. "It's not his fault the manager reported us. The sheriff was nice enough to tell us why Kelsey's mother came here."

Becca sighs. "I don't *dislike* the sheriff. He's just around so much. I'm hardly ever alone with Mom anymore."

My stomach knots. At least Becca knows where her mother is. It's almost noon, and we've only gone to one of the eight addresses. We're not even close to finding Mom. Is she in trouble, waiting to be rescued? Or is she lounging by a hotel pool with her phone shut off?

I must find out.

As I pick up Mom's shoe, I get an idea. I whirl around to my club mates. "We've been going about this all wrong," I say. "Why search with a robot when we can use an experienced tracker that can follow a scent for miles?" I reach for my bike. "Let's go get Major."

Chapter 8

Blackberry Lane

Of course, Leo argues.

"Major already proved he doesn't follow commands." Leo balances with one foot on his gyro-board. "Remember how he just sat there at the junkyard?"

"We weren't using the right words." I kick off on my bike, and we ride out of the apartment complex.

"And he wasn't wearing his work vest." Becca's ponytail ripples behind her as she pedals alongside me. "He proved his skills when he rescued Buggy."

"After he ran away and we had to chase him." Leo rolls between us, his chin jutting out stubbornly. "An animal isn't as reliable as a robot."

"Animals are cute, cuddly, and loyal." Becca increases her speed. "Way better than robots."

I nod. "And we won't look suspicious if we're walking a dog."

"We'll try it your way," Leo says. "But I'm confident you'll discover that robots are better."

After a lunch break at my grandmother's, we pick up Major and the key to his owner's house. The German shepherd seems to know where we're going. He tugs on the leash so excitedly that Leo is almost yanked off his gyro-board.

We coast into Greta's driveway, and my pulse quickens because the last time I was here, I found the elderly woman unconscious on the floor. Thankfully, she's much better now and plans to come home soon.

I unlock the front door.

"Gran Nola said the box is in the hall cupboard." I lead my friends through the living room.

Becca stops to look at a collage of photos arranged on a wall. "Check this out. I think it's Major when he was just a few years old."

I lean in to look at the silver-framed picture of a German shepherd being hugged by a grinning police officer. Major's mouth hangs open like he's grinning too. The officer must be Greta's husband, who passed away a few years after he retired.

We go down the hall and check cupboards until we find one with an oblong box slightly bigger than a shoe box. Inside are leashes, a medal hung on a bright-blue ribbon, a small notebook, and a red padded vest.

"Major has gold bling." Becca dangles the medal from her finger. "The inscription says it's a medal for bravery. Very cool."

Leo lifts the vest. "It's padded but not heavy."

I'm only half listening as I flip open the notebook. It fits in my palm, smaller than my notebook of secrets. Whenever I find out a secret, instead of gossiping, I write it down in my notebook. I used to keep my notebook hidden in a secret drawer of a wooden chest, but my chest, like all our furniture, is in storage. Now my notebook is buried in a drawer under my socks.

This notebook shows all about Major: his American Kennel Club pedigree, date of birth, weight and height chart, training, and vaccination records. I skim through the pages until I come to a list titled Commands.

I look at my club mates in surprise. "No wonder

he wouldn't obey us. These commands are in code."

"Let me see." Leo holds out his hand. I give him the notebook, and he glances through the pages. "Not a code. They're in German."

"Well, he is a *German* shepherd," I say with a smile.

"Does that mean French poodles speak French?" Becca teases.

"Absolutely." My smile widens. "And Japanese spaniels love anime movies."

"Who doesn't?" Becca laughs. "Anime is coolness."

Leo rolls his eyes like he thinks we're silly.

"German is actually very close to English," he explains, tapping his finger on a page of the notebook. "There are thirty commands with pronunciations. *Sitz* obviously is sit, *steh* is stay, and *bringen* is bring. But what does *platz* mean?" Leo takes his mini-tablet from his pocket and brings up a translation page. "*Platz* translates to down." He mouths words to himself as he studies the page, then shuts off his tablet. "I know them now."

I think he's teasing until I notice his serious expression. "But you only read them for like a minute."

Leo nods. "That's all it normally takes to imprint a memory."

Becca and I share an amused glance. Nothing about Leo is normal, which is partly why I like him so much...maybe a lot. I can feel his gaze on me.

"Um, we should go to the second address." I pick up Major's vest and head outside.

Leo consults his phone. "34 Blackberry Lane."

"Blackberry Lane sounds familiar," I say. "Like I heard it recently."

"You did," Leo says as he tucks his phone back into his pocket. "The street name was on a missing-dog flyer your mother gave us last week."

"Oh, I remember." Becca grabs her bike handles. "A year-old dachshund named Cookie. I wonder if she was ever found. I can check the county website to find out."

"We can check missing reports later," I say, eager to get moving. As I hop on my bike, I turn to Leo. "What's the Z code for this report?"

"ZDTHF." He glances up from his tablet. "Becca, do you know what it represents?"

She shakes her head as she kicks off her bike. "Maybe *D* stands for dog."

"Or dangerous," I say with a shiver.

"We'll find out soon." Leo powers up his gyro-board, while holding on to Major's leash.

Blackberry Lane is about three miles away on the west side of Sun Flower, in an upscale development where homes with a lot of land are called *ranchettes*. Large houses in rustic autumn shades blend into the nearby hills. Most of the ranchettes have white-fenced pastures with horses, cows, or even llamas. But there are no animals in the pasture of 34 Blackberry Lane.

Becca points to the metallic-blue Corvette in the driveway. "Check out the cool car. I expected a rancher to have a truck."

"We already have a clue about the people who live here." Leo points to an old-fashioned metal mailbox. On the side, black letters spell out *Barton*.

"The tractor guy could be Mr. Barton," I say, gesturing toward the back pasture. The ground vibrates from the rumble of the tractor's engine, and dirt whirls behind it.

Becca shades her eyes with her hands and peers across the field. "He's busy, but we'll still have to be careful not to be seen. I don't want Mr. Snoopy Sheriff showing up again."

"There aren't many trees or bushes for

camouflage." Leo glances around stealthily. "If we get caught, we'll need a convincing story."

"Or we can tell the truth...at least some of it," I say, thinking quickly. "I'll knock on the door, and if someone answers, I'll say, 'My mother is the animal control officer who came here a few days ago. She may have lost her wallet when she was here and asked me to look for it.'"

"Good ruse," Leo nods. "We'll find out why your mother was here, plus get permission to look around. But Becca should be the one to go."

But this is about my mother, I want to argue. Still, I know Leo's right. We work well together because we have different talents. For anything social, Becca is our girl. She's so genuine that even strangers open up to her.

I watch from the sidewalk as Becca strides confidently up to the front door. She presses a doorbell. I hold my breath. No one answers, so she turns around and comes back to us.

Becca frowns. "No one's home."

"Except Tractor Guy." I gesture toward the pasture.

Leo gazes off with a thoughtful expression. "He can't see us because he just moved behind the barn."

"Time to go spying." I take Mom's shoe from my spy pack and offer the scent to Major, then turn to Leo. "Do you remember the German word for track?"

"Of course." Leo rolls his eyes like I asked him to count to ten. "*Such* means track, and it's pronounced 'tsuuk.'" Leo turns to Major. "*Such!*"

Unlike during the frustrating experiment at Pete's Pick and Pull, Major snaps to attention. He jerks on his leash and whines. I unfasten him—and he's off!

Major lopes up the driveway to the front door, his nose to the ground as if he's caught Mom's scent. He whirls around and runs past the garage to the back of the house and out toward the pasture.

At the fence line, he doesn't even slow down. He squeezes beneath the wood rail and keeps running.

Becca bends down and pokes her hand under the fence. "We won't fit under here like Major."

"So we climb over," I say as I reach up for the top post.

Years of spy practice—pursuing imaginary bad dudes, climbing trees, and hiding in cramped places—have been worth it. I may be short, but I can jump high enough to reach the top of the fence.

I swing over and land smoothly on the other side. Leo lands beside me. And then Becca, but she stumbles as she lands, tumbling to her knees.

She winces as she jumps to her feet. "I'm okay."

"Look!" Leo points. "Major's going to the barn."

Unlike the last barn Major led us to, this one looks brand-new. The outer walls are painted bright red, and there's white trim around the doors and windows. We huddle for a moment to strategize. Running across the pasture is a bad idea because if the tractor guy turns around, he'll see us. We go over to a row of eucalyptus trees that border the pasture and slowly make our way to the barn.

Major barks at a sliding barn door.

"Shush!" I call when I come beside him. "Don't bark!"

Leo and Becca pet the dog, urging him to be quiet. I glance across the field and see plumes of dirt rising from the tractor. The rumble of the tractor's engine covers all other sounds. Safe for now...

"Is the door locked?" Becca asks.

I reach out and twist. "Not locked. I'm going in." And maybe I'll find clues about Mom's disappearance, I think hopefully.

"We'll all go together," Becca says.

Leo nods as he comes up beside us, and we step through the door.

All it takes is a glance to know this isn't like any barn I've ever seen. Instead of farm tools and bales of hay, the room is full of exercise equipment: a treadmill, stationary bike, weights, and other machines.

I let out a low whistle. "My grandmother would love this." Gran Nola is obsessed with yoga and working out.

"No livestock." Becca sounds disappointed. "Why have a barn and pasture if you don't have any animals?"

"He may grow crops," Leo suggests as he goes over to the weight bench. He grunts as he tries to pick up a twenty-pound weight.

"Major must have led us here for a reason." I gaze around the gym-barn in frustration. "You don't call animal control unless there's a problem involving animals, but there aren't any animals. Why did Mom come here?"

Becca snaps her fingers. "The clue is in the Z code. Let's google it!" She pulls out her cell and starts searching. "Here it is," she says excitedly. "ZDTHF stands for dog theft."

"So his dog must have been stolen," I say, deflating. While I feel sorry for anyone who loses a beloved pet, I don't think it's a serious enough crime to bring Mom back here.

I lean against the treadmill, my shoulders slumping. "We won't find anything here. Let's move on."

"Are you sure you don't want to look around more?" Leo asks.

"Or talk to Mr. Barton?" Becca adds.

Before I can answer, Major, who has been sitting quietly, suddenly jumps up. He whines and sniffs the floor.

"He's picked up a scent," Becca says quickly. We follow the German shepherd toward the back of the barn. He stops at a door I'd assumed led to a bathroom.

Leo reaches the door first, but the knob doesn't turn. "It's locked."

"The barn door isn't locked, but this one is?" I point out, suspicious. I lean my head against the wood and hear a soft sound. "OMG!"

Becca grabs my arm. "What?"

"Someone is in there!" I cry softly.

Becca crouches to the crack beneath the door

and peers through the narrow opening. "It's not a big room, probably a closet, and there's a shape... It just moved!"

"What is it?" both Leo and I ask.

"Something small and dark...a dog!"

Not Mom. My heart sinks. But, why is a dog locked in a closet? I think back to Leo's memory of the dog flyer. "Could it be the missing dachshund?" I suggest.

"Maybe." Becca wiggles her fingers under the door. "Here, doggie, come to my hand. Come on, don't be afraid. We're here to help you." Sighing, Becca stands to face us. "She scampered back to a corner. She's terrified. Poor little pup."

Thinking of the dog flyer, suddenly everything makes sense. I gasp. "OMG! We had it backward."

"What?" Leo asks.

"Mr. Barton isn't the victim. He's the thief!"

"No wonder the poor little dog is so scared," Becca says angrily. "We have to get her out of there."

"I can pick the lock with my key spider," I say and reach up for the spy pack on my shoulder.

Leo shakes his head. "No, we can't just take the dog without proof. If we're wrong, we could be accused of stealing. The sheriff should handle this. Becca, will you call him?"

Becca rolls her eyes. "Fine. But let's get out of here first."

We move away from the locked door, and we're halfway across the room when something feels wrong. I stop abruptly. The world has gone quiet. The tractor no longer rumbles.

The front door to the barn creaks, and the tall silhouette of a man looms in the doorway.

He's holding a rifle.

- Chapter 9 -
Surprise Visitors

Although the rifle isn't aimed at us, I tremble as I stare up at the towering stranger. He's rugged and muscled, wearing dusty jeans stained with dried grass and mud. His face is shadowed under the brim of a western hat, but it's obvious he's angry.

He pushes up his hat and glares at us as if we're the bad guys, which is ironic. Someone who imprisons and terrifies a helpless little dog is the worst type of bad guy ever.

"Why are you kids snooping in here?" he growls in a grizzly-bear voice.

I'm too scared to say anything and share anxious glances with my friends. If we all start running past him, can we escape?

"Someone better start talking or else," he warns.

Becca steps forward with a friendly smile, though I know she must be scared too.

"Um...we're so very sorry." She twists her ponytail. "We were out walking our dog, and he ran away so we chased him here." She nods toward Major. "You must be Mr. Barton."

"You know me?" He lifts the brim of his hat to look closer at Becca. "I haven't seen you around here before. You live nearby?"

"Yeah, up the road in the brown house," she says with a vague wave of her hand. All the houses on this street are shades of brown.

"If you kids are here because of the Carters' dog, I already told that animal control lady I don't know where it is." Mr. Barton shrugs. "It's not my fault they let their dog run loose and it got lost."

Liar, liar, I think angrily. And I desperately long to call Mom to tell her we found the dog.

"I don't know the Carters well," Becca says politely. "But I heard that their dog was missing. Why would anyone suspect you?"

"No idea," he says, setting down the rifle. "Don't get me wrong. I have nothing against animals. I especially like fine-looking dogs like your shepherd." He gestures to Major. "He seems well-trained too. Not like that annoying dachshund that kept peeing on my car tires."

"Major's a good dog." Becca moves protectively closer to Major. Bending over, she clips the leash back on his collar.

"German shepherds are smart and powerful dogs." Mr. Barton's gaze sweeps over Major. "Is he trained to attack?"

"Only bad guys," I blurt out with a fierce glare.

"We better go now," Becca says, giving me a warning look. "Sorry to bother you, Mr. Barton. Come on, Major."

I hear Mr. Barton laughing as we scurry out of the barn like scared mice. We don't stop running until we reach the sidewalk.

"That was intense!" Becca blows out a heavy breath. "I was afraid he'd lock us in the closet too!"

Leo wipes sweat from his brow as he hops on his gyro-board. "His evasive manner and facial expressions are evidence of his falsehoods."

"He was definitely lying," I say through gritted teeth. "He stole that dog because it peed on his fancy sport cars. That's sick."

"The sheriff will rescue the dog," Leo says.

"I'll call him," Becca says as she pulls out her phone. She stretches the truth a little, saying we accidentally found the missing dachshund when Major ran into the barn. "He's on his way," she says as she clicks off. "But he warned us not to be here when he arrives."

"Great," I say, relieved that poor dog will be rescued soon. But I'm no closer to finding my mother. I turn to Leo. "What's the next address on the list?"

Leo checks his tablet. "1933 Larkspur Lane with call letters ZWELF."

"What's ZWELF?" I swing up onto my bike.

"Welfare," Becca answers as she reaches for her bike. "Usually it's a complaint about someone mistreating an animal or—" A musical ring interrupts, and she lifts the sparkly pink phone from her pocket. "Mom, what's up? Now? You can't be serious! But I'm not finished...*Fine!*" Becca snaps. Her black eyes blaze as she shoves her phone back into her pocket.

I frown. "That didn't sound good."

"You have to leave?" Leo guesses.

"I have to go home so I can finish my chores and get ready for dinner," Becca says angrily. "As if I need to dress up for *her* date!"

"Drats. I wish you could keep searching with us." I swing onto my bike, ready to take off. "Come on, Leo."

"Actually..." Leo wobbles on his gyro-board. "My aunt is visiting, and I promised I wouldn't stay out too late."

"But we can't give up!" I grip my bike handlebars tightly. "Mom could be hurt and scared."

"Or enjoying a relaxing weekend alone like she texted." Becca reaches across her bike handle to touch my hand. "If she'd been in an accident, she would have called for help. Instead, the texts reassured everyone she was all right."

I try to separate facts and fears as I think about this. If she did leave on her own, why send a few texts, then nothing else? And I can't believe Mom would leave me waiting at school.

"I want to keep looking for her," I say stubbornly. "Can we meet early tomorrow?"

"Absolutely," Leo promises.

"Sure. Unless your mother has returned," Becca says with an encouraging smile. "She could be back by then."

Maybe she's back already, I think with a burst of hope. And suddenly I can't wait to get home.

We make plans to meet early at the third address on Mom's call sheet, then we ride in separate directions.

When I reach my grandmother's house, the driveway is empty and there's a note on the kitchen table from Gran Nola.

Girls' night out with the Red Hat gals.

Tofu casserole in the fridge.

I'd forgotten that she had dinner plans for tonight. I'd told her I didn't mind being alone—and I don't. But the house seems too quiet after I put Major in the backyard. I check the phone for missed messages, crossing my fingers there's news of Mom. Nothing. Once again, I'm disappointed. And when I try to call Dad, it goes to voice mail.

Might as well eat my tofu, I decide with zero enthusiasm. I open the fridge but stop when I hear noise from outside. Before I can investigate, the front door bursts open.

"Surprise!" twin voices shout.

My twin sisters, Kenya and Kiana, rush over to me, laughing as Kenya proudly holds out a large pizza box. They have the same long, dark hair and eyes, but they move and dress so differently that sometimes I forget they're identical. Bold and bossy, Kenya sweeps through life with a dancer's sway, while creative Kiana is more laid-back and is usually nicer to me.

"Check out what we brought!" Kenya calls out as she glides into the kitchen.

"Prehistoric Pizza," I say, smacking my lips. Tofu is okay, but pizza is delish. And I'm really pleased to see my sisters. I've missed them since moving out of the cottage.

"A Saber-Toothed Supreme with everything," Kiana adds, pulling out a chair to sit at the table.

"Kyle got us a discount." Kenya opens the box, and steamy smells make my stomach rumble.

"Was he wearing the costume?" I ask with a grin. My older brother got a part-time job dressing up as a dinosaur at Prehistoric Pizza and didn't tell anyone about it because he was embarrassed.

"He's working behind the counter now," Kiana says as she sets paper plates and napkins on the table.

"Good for him." I sniff the air. "Bacon, cheese, barbecued chicken, and spicy tomato sauce. Yum."

"And plenty of veggies too, for Gran." Kiana glances around. "Her car isn't in the driveway. Where is she?"

"Out with friends. She left me tofu casserole." I gesture to the fridge.

"Well, if you'd rather have tofu..." Kenya teases, pulling back the box.

"No way!" Quick as a blink, I open the box, grab a large cheesy slice, and take a big bite. Sauce drips down my chin, and I wipe it with a napkin.

After I finish my second pizza slice, I glance over at my sisters and catch Kenya mouthing *Are you going to ask her?* to Kiana. I'm glad they don't know I can read lips. Do they have an ulterior motive for coming here? Usually on a Saturday night they're at a party or out with friends. Instead, they're hanging out with their little sister, which is nice but suspicious.

I slap my napkin on the table. "Okay, why are you really here?"

Kiana plucks an olive from her pizza, then smiles at me. "Can't sisters just hang out?"

"We haven't seen you in forever and miss you," Kenya adds.

"Really?" Hope creeps into my voice. It's a cliché,

but as a little sister, I look up to my big sisters.

"Absolutely." Kiana playfully tugs a strand of my hair. "We want to know what's been going on with you. Gran Nola told us you rescued an abandoned puppy. That must have been exciting." She tucks her arm into mine, leading me into the living room.

Kenya sits on the couch, propping a pillow behind her back, then gesturing for me to sit beside her. Kiana plops on my other side so I'm between them. Kenya turns to me. "So tell us about this exciting puppy rescue."

"Major rescued the puppy," I say, smiling. "He ran into a barn and came out with the puppy. She's a tiny thing, no bigger than my fist. Becca named her Buggy because she has adorable big, buggy eyes."

"Is she a pug?" Kiana guesses, pushing back a dark curl.

I nod. "Becca thinks she's a purebred."

"Pugs are adorable!" Kenya bounces lightly on the couch, holding a piece of pizza. "My friend Delainey has been saving forever to buy a pug—I mean, like thousands!—and she's finally going to get one. Delainey says the pup came from champions and will win major dog show awards."

I notice another look pass between my sisters. "But you didn't come here to talk about dogs," I say. "Truth, please."

"Well…" Kenya pauses. "There is something we want to ask you."

"But we didn't want you to think we only came over to get information." Kiana licks pizza sauce from her lips. "I mean, we do miss you. It's horrible how our family is split apart."

"And we're really worried things will get worse. Everything is all messed up." Kenya blinks fast like she's trying not to cry—which surprises me. Soft-hearted Kiana cries easily, but I can't remember the last time I saw Kenya cry.

"That's why we want to find out what you know about Mom." Kiana clasps her hands together. "You were the last one in our family to talk to her. We're worried that something is wrong."

"Finally!" I sag against the couch cushions in relief. "Someone else is worried! I thought I was the only one. I think Mom could be in danger."

"Whoa, Kelsey!" Kenya holds up her hand like a stop sign. "You've been watching too many crime dramas. The only thing in danger is Mom's marriage. That's why we want to know if she told you where she was going or how long she was going to be gone."

"She didn't plan to leave." I shake my head firmly. "She told me she was going to talk to Dad, then move back in with him."

"But she didn't talk to him." Kenya puckers her frosted ruby lips. "Are you sure Mom didn't hint at where she was going? We called all her friends, and no one has seen her."

"That's because she's in trouble." I shake my head. "I don't believe the texts were from her. She promised to pick me up from school, then never showed up—which isn't like her at all."

"Oh, Kelsey," Kiana says with a sad sigh. "I had no idea you were so worried. We should have talked to you sooner...then you'd know."

"Know what?" I ask uneasily.

An unspoken conversation passes between my sisters in brow lifts and nods. Lip-reading was easy to learn, but I never could crack their twin code. Still, I can tell that what they're *not* saying is serious.

After a long silence, Kiana turns back to me with the gravest expression I've ever seen on her face. "Kelsey, we promised Gran Nola we'd never tell... but you need to know the truth."

Kenya nods. "You can't tell anyone. Ever."

"I won't," I promise. "I can keep a secret."
I lean forward to listen.

"Mom and Dad almost got divorced once before."

"No way!" I gasp.

Both of my sisters nod solemnly.

- Chapter 10 -
Sisters and Secrets

"We were just little kids when it happened." Kiana slips an arm around me, her dark hair brushing across my forehead. "But it wasn't until the summer before high school that we discovered our parents were hiding a secret."

"We only found out by accident," Kenya adds as she flips her hair over her shoulder.

"Yeah," Kiana continues in that ping-pong way the twins tell stories. "We were going on a vacation to Canada with our friend Hailey's family, which meant getting passports. Dad offered to fill out our passport applications but needed our birth certificates, so we went up to the attic to get them from the filing cabinet."

Kenya nods. "Dad said to look for a file labeled Family Documents."

"The cabinet wasn't very organized, and we had to look in every drawer." Kiana rolls her eyes. "Finally, we found our birth certificates...but that wasn't all we found."

My sisters exchange somber looks.

In my mystery novels, when secret papers are discovered, they're usually explosive—a shocking will, a long-lost love letter, a treasure map, or a birth certificate for an unknown sibling. OMG! Could I have a sister or brother I don't know about? Am I adopted? Are Dad and Mom my real parents?

"What did you find?" I hold my breath as I wait for the answer.

"Divorce papers," Kenya says bluntly.

My mouth falls open, and I stare at my sisters.

"I don't understand." I dig my fingernails into the couch pillow.

"We were confused too," Kiana says. "Especially when we saw Mom's and Dad's names on the document."

"You mean..." I suck in my breath in shock. "They were divorcing each other?"

Kiana nods, pushing dark hair from her eyes.

"We didn't know what to think, so we went to Dad and showed him the papers. He grabbed them and acted really strange. He told us nothing happened, and it was a mistake."

"Then he shredded the papers," Kenya adds, scowling. "And he told us never to mention it to Mom."

"So of course we went to Gran Nola," Kiana says with a half-smile.

"And she told us what really happened," Kenya adds.

"She explained that while our parents get along great now, they used to argue a lot," Kiana says, shifting on the couch to face me. "One argument was so bad that Mom left us with Gran Nola and drove away without telling anyone where she was going. A few days later, Dad was served with divorce papers."

I twist my hair into a knot. "Our parents are divorced?"

"No." Kiana shakes her head.

"They never filed the papers," Kenya adds.

"Mom came back to Dad because she missed him so much," Kiana continues in a more cheerful tone. "They went to a marriage counselor and learned to talk through their problems instead of arguing. And a year later, you were born." She smiles like this is a fairy tale with a happily-ever-after ending.

Only it isn't.

"Mom is gone again," I say, my heart sinking.

"We're worried too, but we're sure Mom will come back tomorrow." Kiana squeezes my hand. "She's had three days of alone time, so she shouldn't feel stressed anymore. And she works on Monday, so she should be home by Sunday night. She'll talk with Dad, and everything will be fine."

"I hope so," I say softly.

We talk a while longer. Well, mostly my sisters do the talking—gossiping about friends and school drama. I listen, but I'm also thinking about my parents. I can't believe they were almost divorced. If they'd signed those papers, I would never have been born!

After my sisters leave, I go over to the picture wall where my grandmother displays family portraits. I run my fingers fondly over a silver-framed photo of my parents on their wedding day. Mom shimmers in white with daisies in her hair, and Dad looks very handsome in a navy-blue dress suit. They're so obviously in love. Their faces glow as they gaze at each other. It's hard to believe that a few years later, arguments would pull them apart.

Now I understand why Gran Nola doesn't think Mom is in danger and Dad is so angry. Mom has done this before.

For the first time since Mom left me waiting on the curb outside school, I'm not afraid for her safety. I'm angry...and I feel betrayed.

Mom isn't in trouble.

She left to get away from us.

Chapter 11

Larkspur Lane

I wake up from troubled dreams I can't remember, except I know they were about Mom.

It was too late to call Becca and Leo last night, so they don't know the search is off. I jump out of bed to call them, but when I glance at my bedside clock, I groan. We planned to meet at 1933 Larkspur Lane in ten minutes.

Drats! Why didn't I set the alarm?

It's too late to stop them, but if I hurry, I can meet them there. I yank open drawers and toss on jeans and a T-shirt. I start for my closet to get my spy pack...until I realize I don't need it. The CCSC is no longer on a mission. I don't need Major either, so I leave him in the backyard with Handsome.

As I pedal to Larkspur Lane, my shoulders feel light without my spy pack, but my heart is heavy.

What am I going to tell my club mates about Mom? I promised not to talk about the papers my sisters found. I guess I'll just tell them Mom is safe and ask if the sheriff rescued the dognapped dachshund. Then I'll suggest we solve another mystery—like who left Buggy in that run-down barn. I've been so worried about Mom that I forgot about poor little Buggy. How could anyone abandon such a tiny puppy? Or was she lost? The CCSC will find out.

Larkspur Lane isn't far from Sun Flower High, on a quiet street with single-story homes with shady porches squeezed together like cozy friends. I spot my friends on the sidewalk beneath an elm tree and coast over to them.

"Where's your spy pack?" is the first question observant Leo asks.

"I don't need it…not today." Sadness rushes through me as I slide off my bike. "Things have changed."

Becca takes one look at my face and comes over to slip her arm around me. "Kelsey, what's wrong?"

"My sisters came over last night and told me something about Mom." I roll my bike beside

Becca's. "I can't tell you because they swore me to secrecy. But it explains why the adults aren't looking for Mom. You were right, Becca. I should have believed the texts." My heart squeezes as I look into Becca's sympathetic eyes. "Mom doesn't want to be found."

"Are you sure?" Becca asks softly.

I nod. "Mom isn't in danger."

"Well, that's a good thing. She's safe, and you don't have to worry anymore." Becca's tone is cheerful, but she frowns as she studies me. "And there's more good news. Cookie the dachshund was rescued! Sheriff Fischer told me all about it at dinner last night."

"I thought you didn't like him," Leo says in an accusing tone.

"I don't *not* like him. He just annoys me sometimes." Becca flips back her ponytail. "And I'm so glad he returned the dachshund to its owners—even if he didn't have enough proof to arrest Mr. Barton."

"Not enough proof!" I explode, outraged. "The dog was locked inside his barn!"

Becca nods. "You'd think that was enough, but Mr. Barton lied and said he put the dog there to keep it safe until he could find the owners."

"That's illogical." Leo frowns. "He knew the Carters lost a dog."

"We know that, but there's no proof." Becca shrugs. "All that matters is that the dog is back home and soon Kelsey's mom will be too."

"She should be back by tonight." *And then what will happen between Mom and Dad?*

"Let's ride around looking for lost pets." Becca grabs her handlebars. "And afterward we can have a club meeting."

Leo puts his hands on his hips. "I object."

"Object to what?" I turn to him in surprise.

"Quitting." He gives me a disappointed look. "Kelsey, I never expected you to give up on a mystery."

I wince at his words. "I am *not* giving up. I'm being realistic."

"You're ignoring evidence that proves your mother is in jeopardy."

"Trust me," I tell Leo, a bitter taste in my mouth. "Mom left because she wanted to. This isn't the first time she did it."

"Facts don't lie," Leo says with a stubborn jut of his chin. "Fact one: your mother found new information about one of her work calls. Fact two:

she told you she was going to investigate. Fact three: she intended to call your father, yet sent a text instead. Fact four: she didn't pick you up from school despite her promise to you. And according to my observations, your mother would not make a promise she didn't plan to keep."

"Stop already." I shut my eyes to block out the accusing look on Leo's face. "I don't want to talk about Mom anymore."

Leo frowns. "The facts prove your mother needs our help."

"She does *not* want to be found," I insist. "My family is sure she'll be home tonight."

"What if your family is wrong?" He turns slightly to gesture to the house behind us. "We should continue the search, starting with 1933 Larkspur Lane."

I look to Becca for support but she's biting her lip, her gaze darting uncertainly back and forth between us. "I don't know...but maybe Leo is right," she finally says. "It can't hurt to find out why your mom came here."

I shrug, not wanting to argue with my friends. Besides, I *am* curious. But I'm uneasy too, remembering that scary moment when Mr. Barton caught us in his barn. "We have to be more careful this time," I warn.

"And we don't want to look suspicious," Becca adds with a furtive glance around. "Or someone will report us to Sheriff Fischer again."

Leo waves our concerns away with his hand. "I've already contemplated the possible risks and have a strategy prepared to obtain information. I brought this." He holds up a pen with tiny lights spiraling down one side.

"Is that the truth-detector pen you showed me?" I ask.

"The new and improved version. I call it the Poly-Truth 2.0," Leo says proudly. "The red light flashes when the person holding the pen tells an untruth."

Most people would say *lie*, not *untruth*. But Leo is a lot more complicated...and his lopsided smile is cute.

Becca's ponytail brushes against the pen as she bends over for a closer look. "How can a pen detect lies?"

"Yeah, it's so tiny." I run my finger down the pen's red and green lights. "The lie detectors on TV are much bigger."

"This transmits to my tablet," Leo says, a confident gleam in his blue eyes. "When someone holds this pen, their respiration, blood pressure, and skin conductivity are measured through electrodes embedded in the pen."

I don't understand, but I nod like I do. "How do we convince a suspect to hold the pen?"

Leo flashes his crooked grin. "We go undercover."

"Ooh!" A thrill of excitement tingles through me. "Did you bring disguises? What's our cover story?"

"No need for disguises," Leo says with a shrug. "We'll pose as middle-school students."

"That's not a cover," I complain. "That's who we are."

"Precisely why it's a good ruse," Leo says. "We'll ring the doorbell, then say we're students doing a school project and ask them to fill out a form." He zips open his leather pouch and pulls out a clipboard. "There are only three questions. I knew you'd complain if the questions were complex, so they are short and easy to answer."

I read the paper on the clipboard.

Circle the answer that best suits your opinion:
1. How long have you lived in Sun Flower?

    A. 1–5 years

    B. 5–10 years

    C. Longer

2. How many pets do you own?

    A. 1–3

    B. 3 or more

    C. None

3. Which animal do you consider the most intelligent?

    A. Dog

    B. Cat

    C. Bird

"These questions are too random to be useful," I say as I return the clipboard to Leo.

"The questions are unimportant. It's the pen that matters." Leo lifts his chin confidently. "When the suspect holds the pen, Becca will use her social skills to lead up to the important questions, such as why was animal control called to this house? All we know is that the call log had a ZWELF code: concerns for an animal's welfare. But this pen will tell us much more. If the red light flashes, we'll know the suspect is lying. But if the green light stays on, the suspect is being truthful."

Becca leans over to look at the clipboard. "C, B, B," she says. "Those are my answers."

"You don't need to answer." Leo shakes his head. "You're not a suspect."

"I should hope not." She giggles. "But I can't resist answering questions. I like the third one best. Everyone knows cats are the smartest animal."

"Cats are great, but dogs are smarter," I argue. "Major is so smart that he found Buggy."

"You're both incorrect." Leo waves the poly-truth pen at us. "While our kittens are exceptionally smart and Major is a clever dog, it's a known fact that birds have the superior brains. Crows and ravens are highly intelligent and have been known to use logic and multitask."

"Then why are silly people called birdbrains?" Becca teases.

Leo regards her seriously, thinking a moment. "That's an illogical term. Anatomically, a bird has a large brain compared to its head size."

I playfully nudge Becca. "He must be telling the truth because his truth pen is flashing green."

"Facts never lie," Leo says as he hands the clipboard to Becca. "You may ask the questions."

As we near the door, I hold my breath. Each

address we've gone to has led us into trouble. The apartment manager reported us to the sheriff, which was embarrassing. And the last address led us to a rifle-toting dognapper.

I glance around at this ordinary-looking house. The lawn is freshly mowed, and the small bushes beneath the front windows are neatly trimmed. The porch is small, only as wide as the front door itself. I don't get any scary vibes. But someone filed a report about an animal's welfare, so something terrible may have happened here.

Becca clenches the clipboard.

Leo reaches out and presses his finger on the doorbell.

My pulse jumps at the sound of footsteps from within the house...coming closer...closer...

When the door bursts open, I stare up at a tall, blond man wearing dark-green tights, matching green gloves, and a shiny gold shirt that appears to be made of fish scales. And he's holding a three-pronged spike.

Leo gasps. "Aquaman?"

- Chapter 12 -
A Super Pup

When the man chuckles, I realize he's probably in his early twenties. He grins at Leo. "You know your comics."

"I confess to being a fan of DC Comics," Leo says, stepping in front of Becca, who looks as confused as I do. "Your costume is very impressive."

"Thank you. But it's not complete without Mera," he adds, glancing behind him. "I really have to get ready and hurry off to Comic Con, so whatever you're selling, I don't have time to buy any. Sorry."

"We're not selling anything," Becca chirps with a friendly smile. "We're doing a school project and only ask that you answer three questions. They're super short and will only take a few minutes."

"Well…I'm not quite as speedy as the Flash, but I can spare a few minutes. I'm Todd Latoski. And you are?"

"Becca," our social specialist answers, then gestures to me. "She's Kelsey, and that's Leo."

"Nice to meet you kids." When Todd nods at us, his blond hair slips sideways. He reaches up and tugs his wig into place. "So what's this project about?"

"Pets in our community," Becca says and offers him the clipboard. "Just circle your answers."

"We're middle schoolers," Leo puts in as if this isn't as obvious as the wig on Todd's head. "Here, you can use our pen."

"Odd pen," Todd says as he turns the pen in his hands. "Almost looks like a sonic screwdriver. Or maybe you three are really super villains, and this pen is actually a weapon." He looks at us with a grin and a wink. "Should I be careful? Does it shoot laser beams?"

"It's just an ordinary pen," Leo insists with reddening cheeks. He's a terrible liar. If he was holding the pen, it would flash bright red.

Todd chuckles and looks down at the paper. "Hmm…these are easy questions. I've lived here for six years." The pen light flashes green. "I have only one pet, and my dog is much smarter than a cat or bird."

"I believe dogs are highly intelligent," I say with a triumphant look at Leo and Becca.

"My little Mera sure is," Todd says fondly. "She's a natural performer and loves to show off when she has an audience."

There's a tone people use when they talk about animals that clues you in right away that they love animals. Todd is using that tone. What sort of report brought Mom to his house?

"Where's your dog?" Becca asks, glancing past him into the house.

"In the back room. I'd just finished getting her ready for the Con when you rang the doorbell."

This is my chance to find out why Mom came here so I try to keep him talking while he's still holding the poly-pen. "I'd love to meet Mera."

"Me too," Becca adds.

"It's cool you've trained your dog," I add. "I taught mine to sit and stay, but he won't do any tricks. Handsome is sweet and well behaved—unless he sees a squirrel. Then he won't stop barking. Once he barked so much a neighbor complained to Animal Control."

"I know what that's like." Todd sighs.

"Your dog barks too much too?" I ask sympathetically.

"No, but I have a nosy neighbor who called Animal Control on me a few days ago. I love my dog and would never do anything to hurt her. I was so embarrassed when the animal control officer arrived, but she was cool. She looked at Mera and said it was obvious I took good care of my dog."

I'm watching the poly-truth pen in his hand. It glows an honest green, but I suspect there's something he's not telling me.

"Why did your neighbor complain?" I say with a puzzled frown.

"She...um...she didn't approve of Mera's appearance."

"That's outrageous!" Becca puts her hands on her hips. "She has no right to criticize you for how your dog looks. She probably takes her pets to fancy groomers and expects everyone to do the same."

"Actually Mera is groomed regularly...but not in an ordinary way." Todd gestures with his green-gloved hand to a wood-paneled beige house across the street. "Mrs. Craven is probably spying on me right now, and she'll report me again if she sees

Mera. Not that Mera looks bad…It's easier if I just show you."

With a sigh, he turns around and disappears into a back room.

Leo, Becca, and I shift uncertainly on the doorstep, sharing puzzled glances. When Todd returns, he's carrying a very strange-looking dog.

We all stare, our mouths falling open. I have no idea what breed Mera is because she has purple tentacles wiggling around her small body.

"Meet Mera the Octo-Pup," Todd says proudly. "She's the superhero of my new *Octo-Pup* comic book. I'm signing my book at Comic Con, and Mera will sign her paw print. She has thousands of fans and loves wearing her costume. My neighbor thinks it's cruel to put a costume on my dog, but it's very light and as comfortable as a sweater. When Mera knows we're going to a convention, she brings me the costume."

Becca claps and bends down to pet Mera. "She's adorable!"

"What a cute costume." I touch a floppy cloth tentacle.

"A hybrid dog and octopus," Leo adds in an impressed tone. "What are her superpowers?"

"Ink blasts and memory-sucking tentacles." Todd glances uneasily across the street. "I'd love to talk comics with you, but I'm running late and really need to finish packing my car."

"I'll help," Leo offers, and Becca and I offer too.

We carry boxes to a dark-green SUV, and when we finish, Todd opens a box and presents each of us with a comic book with a dramatic cover of Mera. She's wearing her Octo-Pup costume and wrapping a super tentacle around a villainous shark-man. It's cool when Mera dabs her paw on an ink pad and "autographs" our books.

We wave as Todd drives off, and I notice a curtain swaying and a face spying from across the street. The nosy neighbor, I'm sure. Well, she can report Todd if she wants, but my mother won't take her seriously. I remember what Todd said about Mom being cool, and I smile to myself. I don't always understand Mom, but my anger has faded and I just want to see her. I wonder if she's home yet…

"Can I borrow your phone?" I ask Becca as she climbs onto her bike.

"Sure." She hands it to me.

I tap in Gran Nola's number and am relieved when she answers right away. But there's no news of Mom. Not yet anyway.

"So what do you want to do now?" Becca asks as we wheel away from Larkspur Lane.

"I want to talk about finding out who dumped Buggy," I say. "It's a mystery we haven't solved." I feel optimistic because it's Sunday afternoon and in a few hours I'll see my mother. I can't wait to give her a big hug and have our family back together.

"Or we could stop by one more address," Leo says as he looks up from his tablet. "According to the map, Vine Road is on the ride back to your gran's house."

"Are you sure?" I ask, puzzled. "I don't remember a road with that name."

"It's off Grove Street, halfway between Pete's Pick and Pull and your grandmother's house. It won't take long to check it out."

"But it would be a waste of time." I shake my head. "There's no reason to follow Mom's trail anymore. She'll be home tonight."

Leo frowns but doesn't argue.

After we pass Pete's Pick and Pull and turn onto Grove Street, I pay close attention to the street signs. I've ridden this way a zillion times, so why haven't I seen Vine Road? Could Leo's map be wrong?

Abruptly, Leo stops by a country road half-hidden between thick trees. Becca and I slow to a stop while Leo spins around on his gyro-board to face us. I look up for a street sign, but there isn't one.

My heart races like I'm running a marathon, only I'm standing still. And I get a strange déjà vu feeling as I look down the familiar dirt road.

Three days ago, Leo, Becca, and I were here.

It's where we found Buggy.

Chapter 13

Vine Road

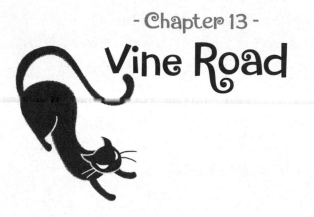

"Why did Mom come to a deserted road?" I stare down the narrow dirt road where stalks of wheat stretch into the horizon. "There aren't any houses."

"The only building is the broken-down barn." Becca balances on her bike as she points toward the dead end.

Leo shades his eyes with his hands to peer off in the distance. "If no one lives here, who called in the ZABAND report?"

"ZABAND must mean an abandoned dog!" Becca says excitedly. "Maybe someone out for a walk or driving by heard Buggy barking."

"But Mom didn't find Buggy," I say with a puzzled glance around. Could Vine Road be where

Mom went that seemed like a routine call until she learned new information?

Pursing my lips, I remember Mom asking where we'd found Buggy. When I'd described the old barn, locked gate, and no-trespassing sign, Mom said, "I think I know the place."

Of course, she knew! She'd been here the day before. When she told me she had new information about a call, I thought she'd found it on the job. But she found out about Buggy at home—from *me*!

And she'd planned to come back to investigate Friday morning—but did she? And if she did, what did she find?

I kick off on my bike pedal. "Let's go to that barn," I shout over my shoulder as I zoom down Vine Road.

"Slow down!" I hear Becca calling behind me. "Wait for us!"

But I don't wait—I pedal faster.

Questions whirl at superspeed in my head. How did Buggy end up in the barn? Did she wander away from her owners? Was she abandoned or stolen? Buggy is too tiny to wander this far away from a house, and a pug is too valuable to be abandoned. If she'd been stolen, Mom would have returned her to her rightful owner instead of allowing Becca to take her home.

Where did Buggy come from?

When I slam on my brakes at the dead end, dust whirls up and makes me cough. Becca and Leo roll up beside me, and we all stare beyond the no-trespassing sign posted on the rickety gate.

"Don't even think about going inside," Becca warns with a sharp look at me.

"I'm not even sure *how* to get inside." I study the caved-in roof, collapsed door, and boarded-up windows. "But Major did."

"A dog can squeeze into places that wouldn't be safe for us," Becca says.

"According to my observations, the structure is too hazardous to enter." Leo props up his gyro-board against a wooden post. "But we can climb over the fence and explore the perimeter of the barn."

I bite my lip as I stare at the caved-in roof. "What if someone's trapped inside?"

"Do you mean your mom?" Becca asks softly.

"I don't know...maybe." My voice cracks as I imagine Mom trapped beneath wooden beams, unconscious. "I really think Mom will come home tonight, but finding out she came here on a call is too much of a coincidence. I have to look."

"We'll investigate." Leo narrows his gaze at the gate. "Unfortunately, you neglected to bring your spy pack, so we don't have the key spider to pick the lock. But the gate will be easy to climb over. Allow me to go in first to inspect the area."

"No." I pull him back as he starts to climb. "I don't want you to get hurt."

"Nice to know," he says with a lopsided grin.

"I didn't mean..." I jerk my hand off his arm, my cheeks burning. "We need to make sure it's safe before anyone goes in."

"Agreed, and we should let an adult know where we are," Becca says, coming up beside me. She pulls out her cell and bends over the tiny keyboard. "I'll text Mom."

"Good idea," I say. Then I turn back to Leo.

He offers me his hand. "Would you like a boost over the gate?"

My cheeks are still hot from touching his arm, so I shake my head, hurry past him, and jump to grasp the top of the fence. I may be short, but I can jump high. I'm over the fence first. Leo and Becca land beside me.

We rush to the barn. One side is caved in so the roof slants to the ground. The barn was probably painted brown when it was first built, but now it's a crumbling dust color. The doorframe has shattered into splinters. I walk around, stepping over weeds and broken boards, searching for a way in.

"Over here!" Leo calls.

I follow his voice around to the side of the barn where a glassless window frame yawns open into darkness. This must be how Major got inside!

I cup my hands around my mouth and call into the black hole, "Hellooooo! Is anyone in there?"

I tilt my head and listen…Nothing.

"Is anyone there?" I call louder this time. "Anyone?"

Again, there's no reply.

Leo taps me on the shoulder, and I look into his somber face. "Your mother isn't here," he says softly.

"She could have come to search for clues about Buggy after she left the animal shelter," I say with growing fear.

"So where's the truck?" Leo asks. "If she was here, it would be parked by the gate. But there aren't any vehicles on this road."

He makes logical sense, but I can't shake my fear.

"Mom would have risked her life to help an animal," I say, unable to take my gaze off the barn. "I know there are lots of reasons to think she's okay, but there are reasons to wor—"

"Clues!" Becca interrupts with a squeal. "Come look!"

"What?" Leo and I turn to stare at her.

"Prints in the dirt." She points to the ground.

I shrug. "There are probably lots of paw prints from wild animals."

"I recognize the tiny long ones," Leo says, bending down to study the ground. "Those are raccoon."

"Not animal prints." Becca's ponytail flops as she shakes her head. "Shoe prints!"

I squint at where she's pointing and see wavy shapes in the damp dirt. "That curvy line could be a heel," I say.

"And there's another one over here," Becca adds excitedly. "Only it's bigger."

"Excellent clue, Becca." Leo takes out his phone and snaps photos of the ground. "According to my calculations, the larger print is 11 inches, and in the United States, the average female foot is 8.5, so this print is probably from a man's shoe. The smaller print, though, is approximately six inches, which indicates a woman's shoe."

"A leather work boot," I guess in a hushed tone.

"Perhaps." Leo nods. "I'll know more when I analyze the photos on my home computer."

I bend down and compare the dirt prints against my foot. I inhale sharply because the length is identical. Mom and I both wear size six.

Before I can say anything, Becca calls out, "Hey, I found more imprints—but they aren't animal or human."

Leo and I hurry to the side of the barn where she's pointing at a muddy patch. "There's something familiar about this print, even though it's weird," Becca says. "A big square of crisscross marks."

"Tiny squares like graph paper," Leo adds.

I'm only half listening, still thinking about the Mom-sized boot print. Now more than ever, I'm sure Mom was here.

"I know what it is!" Becca's shrill voice snaps me back to attention. "It's a cage print!"

"Not a very big cage," Leo says skeptically.

"But big enough to hold a little dog," I say ominously.

Leo's blue eyes widen. "Could it have been used

to transport Buggy?"

"Yeah—and maybe other dogs too." Becca turns to me. "Kelsey, do you have any idea why your mother would come here?"

I bite my lip as I remember my last conversation with Mom. "She mentioned shutting down a puppy mill and a dogfighting ring, but that happened last month."

"Mr. Barton acted really suspicious," Becca points out. "Maybe he stole other dogs. If we can prove he's involved in more animal crimes, Sheriff Fischer can arrest him."

"We don't have any proof to suspect him," Leo says.

"Can we just get out of here?" Becca shudders. "This place gives me the creeps."

"Not before I see what's inside." I point through the black-hole window into the barn. "Leo, do you have a flashlight?"

"I do." Leo glances at the pouch he has slung over his shoulder. "But I'm not giving it to you."

"Come on, Leo. Hand it over." I hold out my palm. "I just want to shine a light through the window."

"You promise not to go inside?" he asks suspiciously.

"I just want to make sure no one is trapped in there," I say, hoping he doesn't notice I didn't answer his question.

When he gives me a tiny flashlight pen, I thank him, then aim the beam through the frame of the broken window. Shining the beam back and forth, I can see that only half of the barn is crushed. Rotten wooden boards dangle from the caved ceiling to the dirt floor. I reach deeper into the hole, inhaling musky odors, probably from wild animals. The beam catches the flash of tiny eyes, and something small scurries under a woodpile. Too small for a skunk, maybe a rat—and where there's one rat, there probably are dozens more. I should click off the light, turn around, and leave.

But my light glints off something white far in the back. It's about the size of my hand and snagged by a pile of debris. Clothing? Paper? I can't tell from this far away, and curiosity ripples through me.

I glance back at my friends. Becca is pointing to more footprints in the dirt, and Leo is snapping pictures. Before they can tell me not to do something stupid, I hold my breath and jump through the hole.

- Chapter 14 -
Buried in the Barn

I land on a broken board that wobbles; my feet slip, and I tumble onto the hard dirt. Wincing, I wipe my stinging hands on my jeans. As I stand, I bump my head. *Ouch!* Swiveling the flashlight upward, I see a dangling wooden beam hanging inches in front of my face. This whole barn is just a sneeze away from collapsing. I have to be quick.

"Kelsey!" Becca cries out. "Are you okay?"

"Yeah." I blink away dust to see Becca's and Leo's concerned faces framed in the glassless window.

"Come back before you hurt yourself," Leo urges.

"I will after I check something"—I cough from the smell of musty dirt and hay—"over there."

I aim the flashlight's beam on the white,

unnaturally shiny object among the wooden debris. Cautiously, I step over shattered boards, waving the beam wide around what's left of the barn. Nothing moves except my shadow, which wavers in the flashlight's glow.

Following the beam, I bend over to pick up a square of paper.

"Only paper," I call out to my friends.

Becca shouts for me to hurry back, but I'm puzzling over the paper.

It's shiny and crisp, instead of wrinkled and filthy like I would've expected. Did it blow in through the broken window, or was it dropped? I shine my flashlight in a wide arc around the barn. The beam sweeps low across the dirt-covered wooden floor, and I stare in surprise—more cage imprints!

The crisscross marks are like the ones we found outside. I count three small cages and a jumbo-sized one. Proof that animals—dogs?—were kept in this barn. Was Buggy in one of the cages? But if so, how did she get out? Why was she left behind?

I squint at the paper. Even with the flashlight, the small print is hard to read in the dark. I can barely make out the bold words at the top of the paper: Certified Pedigree.

Carefully, I make my way back to my friends. When I lift my arms, Leo gently pulls me through the window frame and onto the ground. "Thanks," I say, my cheeks warming.

Leo frowns. "You shouldn't have risked your safety."

"I'm fine." I blink at the bright sunlight and brush off my jeans, wincing at the pain in my palms.

"Are you injured?" His tone softens.

I shake my head. "Just some scrapes."

"Kelsey, what were you thinking?" Becca storms over, her glossy peach lips pressed together in annoyance. "You're lucky the roof didn't fall on you. And you're a mess, covered in dirt and... Yuck, a spiderweb." She plucks a silvery strand from my hair.

"I'll fix my hair later. Look what I found." I wave the paper like a prize. "A clue!"

"You risked being buried in the barn for a piece of paper?" Becca asks with a disapproving frown.

"It's a document and may be important. See how shiny it is? Like someone dropped it recently— maybe Mom. I think the small shoe prints belong to her." I swallow hard. "And I found four cage prints inside, including a really large one."

"More cages?" Becca's dark eyes widen. "That proves animals were kept here! I'll bet it was that horrid dog thief Mr. Barton."

"The footprints are large enough to be his," I point out. "Although I don't think he's involved in this."

"May I have the paper?" Leo holds out his hand to me. "Certified Pedigree," he reads out loud. "American Ken—"

"American Kennel Club," Becca interrupts with an excited jump. "I saw lots of those forms when Mom was raising Yorkies. Purebred dogs register with the AKC and usually have a lineage of champion parents and grandparents. It's a big deal for dog shows."

"Finding this paper has to be more than a coincidence." I rub my chin thoughtfully. "But why would anyone keep dogs in a broken-down barn?"

All of our clues lead to more questions. Mom was called out to this barn because someone probably heard barking. But she didn't find anything. Does that mean the dogs that were kept here had been moved? When we found Buggy the next day, Mom was *very* interested. She confided to me that she planned to investigate something suspicious in the morning. Did she come back here?

"Peculiar word combinations." Leo furrows his brow as he runs his finger down a column on the paper. "Black Bart's Mini Burrito, Sabrina's Sweet Oreo, and Opalina Dancing Dandelion. Are these cryptic codes or a food menu?"

Becca bursts out laughing. "They're dog names."

"You're joking." Leo eyes her doubtfully.

"Cross my heart." She makes a crisscross gesture across her chest. "Pedigreed dog names are coolness."

I peer over Leo's shoulder. There are columns with names in brackets like the family tree project I did in English. Leo's right—the names are peculiar. I look up at Becca. "Someone really named a dog Precious Spooky Sapphire?"

Becca nods. "Fancy-schmancy names for fancy-schmancy dogs. Mom and I used to laugh at some of the registered names. I remember one that was like a tongue twister: Princess Penelope of Pineapple Palace. Try saying that fast three times."

"No thanks." I roll my eyes. "And I thought naming my dog Handsome was strange."

"The names get even crazier when the pups are bred from champion sires or dams because the breeders usually give long names from their champion lineage," Becca adds. "This pedigree shows the pup's name is Pearl's Daring Bartimus, and the names of her parents and grandparents are listed too."

I point excitedly. "Check out the breed—a pug! This must be Buggy's pedigree!"

"Au contraire." Leo taps his finger on the paper. "You're overlooking one important detail on this pedigree."

I follow Leo's gaze and read the tiny printed words:

PEARL'S DARING BARTIMUS

PUG MALE BLK

I gasp. "Male?"

"No way." Becca shakes her head vehemently. "I've bathed Buggy, and she's definitely a girl. It must be a typo and should read *female*."

"But that's not the only discrepancy," Leo says in his know-it-all tone. "Read the physical description."

Becca's lips move slightly as she reads. "BLK is an abbreviation for black, but Buggy is mostly brown with black markings. Three months old? Buggy isn't more than six weeks." Becca looks up with a puzzled expression. "This isn't Buggy's pedigree."

"Precisely." Leo nods.

"Now I'm really confused." I rub my forehead.

Becca hands the paper back to Leo. "Something suspicious was definitely going on here. Sheriff Fischer needs to know about this. He's probably still at my house. We should show him the pedigree."

Leo shakes his head. "I want to keep the pedigree for further investigation."

"But telling the sheriff what we found is a good idea. You go talk to him, Becca," I say, suddenly weary. "I just want to talk to Mom. If she's not back yet, she will be soon, and then I'll ask her about this barn."

"I'll analyze our clues when I get home." Leo zips the pedigree into his leather pouch. "I'll let you know what I find out."

We don't say much as we leave the barn, climb over the gate, and ride down the rutted road. When my friends turn right, I pedal left for Gran Nola's house. As I pass the houses, I think of how much I want to see Mom. I miss her a lot. And I have lots of questions to ask her about the dogs...and Dad. I need to know that she and Dad are okay.

I'm disappointed her work truck isn't in the driveway, but it's not even noon yet. Mom will probably return late this afternoon.

When I step into the house, Gran Nola glances up from the couch where she's reading a yoga magazine. Disappointment crosses her face, and I know she'd hoped to see Mom too.

"Have you heard anything?" I ask, sitting beside her.

"Not yet." My grandmother closes her magazine, setting it on the coffee table beside her cell phone. Her gaze lingers on the phone, then shifts back to me. "Are you hungry? I'll make you lunch."

"I'm not hungry." I glance at the dark screen of the phone. "Have you tried calling again?"

"Only about a million times." Gran Nola sighs. "She'll come home when she's ready."

"I hope it's soon. Maybe she...What was that?" I touch my ear and glance toward the door. "I think I hear a car."

"I don't hear any...Oh! It does sound like a car!" Gran Nola jumps up.

"Or maybe a truck!" I spring over to the window,

push back the curtain, and peer through the glass at the driveway.

My shoulders sag. Not Mom's truck but the secondhand Honda my brother sometimes borrows from a friend. And Kyle isn't alone. My sisters pile out of the backseat.

"Pizza delivery!" Kyle calls out as he briskly strides inside, his arms full of two large boxes. He has the same wavy brown hair as my sisters and is wearing his Prehistoric Pizza shirt. "I couldn't concentrate at work," he says with a sigh. "So when the twins said they wanted to come here, I grabbed two unclaimed pizzas and we all came together."

"Kiana and I have been texting with Kyle, Dad, and Gran Nola all morning," Kenya adds. "Hearing no news is frustrating, so we decided to wait with you."

"I never say no to pizza." I sniff the pizza boxes. "Do I smell barbecue sauce and bacon?"

"Taco Fiesta and Barbecued Triple Meat." Kyle spins the pizza boxes on his fingertips like they're basketballs.

Suddenly I'm hungry. We grab paper plates and napkins. Gran Nola pours glasses of iced tea.

We're together again like a family...almost.

One pizza has already been devoured when there's a text ding from my grandmother's cell phone. She hurries to answer it as I take my glass to the sink.

Gran Nola gasps.

The glass almost slips from my fingers, but I catch it and set it down.

Whirling around, I rush over to my grandmother. She taps her phone screen, her eyes wide and anxious.

"It's from your mother," she says.

- Chapter 15 -

Message from Mom

I take a deep breath, then read the text.

I'm fine.

Don't try to find me.

I'll be back in a few days.

And that's all she wrote. No explanation, just the short message with no emotion. Has my mother become a robot?

My grandmother rereads the text, her lips drawn into an angry frown. And when I glance over to the couch, my sisters are wearing identical expressions of hurt and anger as they stare at their phone.

"We got the same text," Kenya says, her words dropping like crushing stones.

"Me too," my brother says as he walks in from the kitchen, his phone in his hand. "I don't know what's going on with Mom, but I don't like it."

"At least she's okay," Gran Nola says with forced optimism.

"She may be, but we aren't," Kiana says bitterly. "This text doesn't even sound like Mom."

Maybe she didn't send it. But then who? And why? If someone else really did send the message, that means Mom is in danger. Has she been kidnapped?

"Your mother is going through a difficult time," my grandmother tells Kiana. She holds my sister and lightly kisses her forehead. "We have to support her. I'm sure she'll explain when she's ready."

I feel so helpless. There isn't anything I can do. Only wait, which is how this all started...when I waited at school for a mother who never showed up. Is Mom in trouble, or did she really leave because she wants a divorce? She told me that losing the cottage caused problems between her and Dad. We'd still be living there if I hadn't helped find Mr. Bragg's lost family. So it's all my fault.

My throat tightens, and I blink back tears. I mumble some excuse and go to my room.

My orange kitten, Honey, is curled against my pillows. I scoop her up in my arms and hold her so tightly that she squirms. I ease my grip but don't let go. Tears fall on her orange fur and she stops squirming, as if she understands that I need her.

There are reminders of Mom all around the room—her suitcase, her sneakers, and the family photo propped on my dresser of a trip to Disneyland when we were a complete family of six. Will we ever be a complete family again? Or is Mom going to divide us into fractions?

I don't know how long I huddle on my bed, hugging my cat and staring at the family photo. When I hear ringing from the living room, I jump and Honey flies from my lap.

I race down the hall as the phone rings again. Gran Nola grabs it with a shaky hand, and my siblings and I gather around her like a family hug to listen.

"Katie?" Gran Nola cries, hope shining in her eyes. "Oh." She blows out this single word like it's a pin popping a balloon.

"Who is it?" my brother asks softly, slipping his arm around her.

"Not Katie." Gran holds out the phone to me.

"For you."

I don't want to take it, especially with everyone staring at me as if I've done something wrong. But what else can I do except lift the phone to my ear? "Uh...hello," I say awkwardly.

"Kelsey!" Leo says excitedly. "I've been analyzing the pedigree you found, and you'll never guess what I discovered!"

"Um...this isn't—" I try to say, but he doesn't pause to listen.

"While the canine pedigree names are legitimate, the certificate is fake," Leo rushes on. "The mother dog died seven years ago, so obviously she couldn't have had a litter three months ago. Forging fake champion lineages for unregistered puppies could be very profitable. I suspect the barn was a puppy mill. We need to discuss this right away. I've already called Becca, and she's on her way over. How soon can you get here?"

I hear what he's saying, but my brain is stuck on numb. I don't care about forged pedigrees or a puppy mill. I just want to hear Mom's voice. Why did it have to be Leo on the phone instead of her?

"No!" I say sharply. "I can't come over."

"Why not? Are you eating dinner?"

"No...I just can't...." I sweep my gaze around at my sisters, brother, and grandmother. They're all staring at me.

"Did I do something to anger you?" Leo asks in a hurt tone.

I open my mouth, but nothing comes out. I can't explain this to him. Talking about it might mean it's real and that Mom is leaving our family.

So I hang up.

Hanging my head, I murmur *sorry* to my family and escape to my room.

When I fling myself on my bed, Honey mews a complaint, then jumps to the floor. I bury my face in my pillow. Just then, the door opens and I blink up at the sister-sized shapes in the dark.

"Scoot over," Kiana says in a weary voice.

"Don't hog the whole bed," Kenya adds in a whisper. The mattress jostles, and I'm pushed over. "Gran Nola said we could stay here, so we're sleeping with you."

"We would have slept on the couch bed, but Dad had already claimed it," Kiana adds with a yawn.

"Dad's here?" I squish my pillow and try to get comfortable, but an elbow pokes in my side.

"He got a text too—same one we did—and came over to be with us." Kenya yanks the sheet away from me. "He's really upset, but Gran Nola is calming him down."

I squeeze my eyes shut tightly and bury my face in my pillow. Not long ago the biggest problem in our family was losing the cottage. But houses can be replaced.

When I start to sob, an arm reaches across the blankets to pat my shoulder. "It'll be okay, Kelsey," Kiana whispers.

I want to believe her, but all I can think about is Mom.

Usually Monday mornings are a hectic rush of getting dressed, gulping down breakfast, and hurrying to school before the bell rings. But I wake up feeling sick to my stomach, and Gran Nola says I can stay home. I crawl back in bed and sleep for a few more hours.

When I wake up again, I hear Gran Nola's yoga music and voices coming from the workout room. I wander into the kitchen. No one is there, so I guess my siblings went to school and Dad is at work.

I pour myself some orange juice and heat up a blueberry muffin. My gaze drifts over to Gran's phone charging on the counter, and last night rushes back to me. Mom's text.

Don't try to find me.

I tell myself not to think about her as I wipe crumbs off my hands and toss the crumpled napkin away.

I go into the living room and turn on the TV. But my thoughts keep drifting from Mom and the text to how horribly I treated Leo. I shouldn't have hung up on him. I'll call when school's over and apologize.

What was Leo trying to tell me? Oh yeah, the pedigree certificate was a fake, and the barn may have been used for a puppy mill.

Is that why Buggy was found there? I wonder as I lean back on the couch.

I don't know much about puppy mills except that dogs are overbred, starved, and squeezed into dirty cages, which is why Mom and the sheriff shut them down.

Does this mean there's another puppy mill in Sun Flower?

Puzzling over a mystery instead of worrying about Mom is a relief, so I borrow Gran Nola's cell phone and do a search. I find a list of five puppy mill facts:

1. A puppy mill is a breeding kennel that usually produces dogs in cramped, filthy conditions for resale.
2. Puppy mill dogs are bred for quantity, not quality.
3. Pet shops often buy dogs from puppy mills.
4. Overbreeding leads to malnutrition, sickness, and unsociable dogs that often end up abandoned.
5. Puppy mill kennels can consist of anything from tethers attached to trees to cages made of wood and wire mesh.

Wire-mesh cages! Like the crisscross imprints we found at the barn. And if the puppy mill breeders forged pedigrees, they could charge a lot for each puppy. I search through websites about champion-bred pug puppies and learn they sell for two thousand to five thousand. Multiply that by dozens—maybe hundreds—of puppies, and the payoff would be huge.

Huge enough to try to stop someone from interfering.

When I told Mom where I'd found Buggy, she must have gone back to the barn to investigate and see if she'd missed something.

Did she track down the new location of the puppy mill?

Did she confront the bad guys?

And did they do something drastic to stop her?

I rush out of my room to call Sheriff Fischer.

- Chapter 16 -
Pedi-Greed

Sheriff Fischer doesn't answer. My call is passed over to Deputy Phil, a skinny, rude guy who doesn't like kids. He tells me the sheriff is out of the office.

"I'm really busy here, but I'll tell him you called," Deputy Phil adds impatiently.

When he hangs up, I fight the urge to throw the phone across the room. The more I think about Mom leaving without calling Dad or taking her suitcase or answering her phone, the more I'm sure she's been kidnapped. While I was waiting at school for Mom to pick me up, she was waiting too—waiting to be rescued. But I can't find her on my own. I need my club mates.

Becca can't resist checking her phone during

breaks or when the teacher isn't looking. I send a text from my grandmother's cell phone:

CM OVR L8R w/Leo

TELL HIM SORRY

I click Send.

Within minutes I get a reply.

OK

CU L8R

I escape into the backyard and toss a Frisbee to Handsome and Major. As I throw the Frisbee over and over, I try not to worry. Instead, I think about how to find the puppy mill. Buggy is enough proof that it must still be operating. If we can somehow find the location of the mill, maybe we can find my mom.

Something Kenya said pops into my mind. A friend of hers—Deanne? No Delainey—is buying a champion-pedigreed pug. Is it a coincidence that after years of saving for a purebred pug, Delainey found one at the same time a puppy mill may be operating in Sun Flower?

I go into the house to use Gran Nola's phone to text Kenya. But my plans change when I find Kenya in the kitchen, opening up the fridge. I don't know why she's here instead of at school, but I'm thrilled to see her. With her earbuds blasting out music loud enough for me to hear, she doesn't notice I'm standing behind her until I tap her shoulder.

Kenya gives a startled gasp and tugs off her earbuds. "Kelsey, don't sneak up on me like that."

"I need to ask you something," I say quickly. "It's important."

"Lower your voice." She touches her finger to her lips as she points into the living room where Kiana is sleeping on the couch. "What do you want?"

"You said your friend Delainey bought a pug puppy?" I whisper.

"Not yet. It was supposed to be delivered today, but there was a travel delay."

"Where's it coming from?" I ask.

"Tennessee." Kenya wags a finger at me. "But don't even think about buying one. They're crazy expensive—over a thousand dollars per dog."

"No worries. I prefer big dogs like Handsome," I reply.

"Delainey says she's getting a good deal. She's added to her puppy fund for years by creating websites for her parents' friends." Kenya twirls her earbuds on her finger. "She's been obsessed with pugs since she was little and her grandparents took her to a dog show. It's her dream to compete in dog shows."

If I'm right, she's going to be very disappointed, I think sadly.

"I need to talk to Delainey right away," I tell my sister.

"Why?" She raises her brown brows. "You don't even know her."

I look solemnly into her face. "Delainey may help us find Mom."

"Don't be crazy. She only met Mom once. And she doesn't know anything about what's going on."

"But she may know something important. Trust me on this. I'm going to find Mom. That's why I need to talk to Delainey."

"I think you're bonkers. But whatever, it can't hurt. Go talk in the bedroom so you don't wake Kiana. She didn't sleep well last night and needs to rest." Kenya taps on her phone. "Hey, Delainey, this may seem weird, but my little sister wants to talk to you."

She tosses the phone to me, and I catch it.

"Delainey?" I say uncertainly.

"Yeah...?" She sounds puzzled, her voice honey sweet with a southern twang.

"I'm Kelsey, the youngest sister." I lower my voice as I go down the hall to the guest bedroom. "We haven't met, but I need to ask you something."

"Are your sisters okay?" Delainey interrupts, sounding worried. "Kenya and Kiana seemed really quiet at school, and then they left early."

"They're fine, just some family stuff going on." I take a deep breath, then rush on before Delainey can ask more questions. "Kenya told me you're buying a pug. Can you tell me about it?"

"Luna isn't mine yet." Delainey's tone rises excitedly. "I can't wait to meet her! She's so tiny with the sweetest black, squishy nose."

"She sounds adorable. How did you find her?"

"From a breeder online," she says. "Why? Do you want to buy a pug too?"

"Who wouldn't? They're so adorable. But we already have a dog." I think fast as I sit on the bed. "I'm asking because a friend of mine wants a purebred pug. It's her dream to raise a puppy she can enter in dog shows."

"Me too!" Her voice warms like we're suddenly best friends. "Usually champion-sired pups are over four thousand dollars, but I'm getting Luna for half-price. I thought I'd have to wait another year to buy one, but then I found out about Merry Lee Vandameer from an online pug discussion group."

"Who's she?" I lean forward on the edge of the bed.

"Only one of the most respected breeders of champion pugs in the world. Mrs. Vandameer is the nicest lady ever, and she was born in Tennessee just like me! Isn't that a cool coincidence?"

"Yeah." *If it's true.*

"She cares more about finding a good home for her dogs than making a profit. Luna will do great in dog shows," Delainey adds in a dreamy tone. "And I'll use the prize money to pay for college. It's a win-win."

Or a lose-lose if Luna's pedigree is fake. I want to warn her, but I don't have any proof...yet.

"Sounds like a great deal," I say, trying to sound impressed instead of suspicious. "Especially for a champion-bred pup. She must have an impressive pedigree. Have you seen the certificate?"

"Yeah, and it's awesome. The pedigree goes back to Luna's great-great-great grand-champion parents. Her full name is Legendary Queen Luna of Peltier Palace, and she's the most perfect puppy in the world."

"But are you sure it's a real pedigree?" I ask. "I

read this article online about forged pedigrees. You have to be really careful."

"I'm very careful," Delainey says. "I insisted on knowing all about Luna's lineage. Mrs. Vandameer told me I was smart to be cautious and sent me photos of Luna's parents and grandparents with blue ribbons and trophies. She has five grand champions in her lineage."

"Wow, that sounds too good to be true! Do you think she'd give my friend a good deal too?"

"Sure, especially if you say I referred you."

"What's her number?" I glance around the bedroom for a pen and paper but don't see any. I walk into the connecting bathroom and tear off a square of toilet paper and grab a dark-brown eyebrow pencil from my sisters' makeup bag.

I write down the numbers as Delainey recites them, the dark-brown pencil smearing across the tissue like sloppy crayon art. "Thanks," I say as I toss the eyebrow pencil back in the makeup bag. "My friend is going to be so excited."

"Tell her to check out the website, Vandameer's Premier Pugs. There's a list of pugs for sale and photos of happy owners holding their pups. And my photo will be added after Merry Lee delivers Luna."

"When is the delivery?"

"Tomorrow!" she sings out happily. "I can't wait to hold my darling pug baby. I already have a plush doggy bed and chew toys for her and...Oh! The bell rang! I've got to get to my next class!"

After we hang up, I stare at the phone's dark screen and hope I'm wrong about Luna.

One way to find out. I do a quick search on my sisters' phone.

The Vandameer's Premier Pugs site pops up with puppy photos. Squishy black faces and big eyes just like Buggy's stare out from the screen. There are rave reviews from satisfied buyers and a long list of impressive awards. Lots of pug photos, but I can't find any of Merry Lee Vandameer. And the only contact info is the phone number Delainey gave me. Is the site legitimate?

I'm scrolling through puppy photos when I hear the faint ring of a phone in another room. A moment later my grandmother steps into the bedroom, holding the phone out to me. "It's for you," she says, a puzzled look on her face.

"Who is it?" I ask, shoving my sisters' cell into my pocket.

My grandmother frowns. "The sheriff."

Chapter 17

Puppy Pondering

"My deputy said you called," Sheriff Fischer says, sounding tired.

"Yeah." I hesitate because my grandmother is watching me curiously. When she turns and leaves the room, I blurt out, "I know where Mom went on Friday!"

"What have you been up to?" His tone sharpens.

"Searching for Mom." I pause. "Someone had to."

"Kelsey, we've been over this before. There's no evidence to indicate she's in danger of anything except losing her job if she doesn't have a good reason for missing another day of work."

"She has a good reason. She's in trouble." I pace on the carpet, too tense to sit down. "She went on a call to Vine Road on Wednesday, and I'm sure it's where she returned Friday morning."

"Vine Road? I remember that address from her call sheet—a report of an abandoned dog. But your mother didn't find any animals."

"That's where my friends and I found Buggy in an old barn."

"The little pug Becca is caring for?"

"Yeah. We think the barn was used for a puppy mill and Buggy escaped. When Mom found out about Buggy, she must have gone back Friday morning to investigate."

"But she didn't go out on any calls," he says. "And the only puppy mill I know of was shut down last month."

"Did you arrest the bad guys?"

"Unfortunately, laws aren't tough on animal crimes. The Midgley brothers were fined, and we confiscated about a dozen Pomeranians and poodles. If they're caught breeding dogs illegally again, they'll be arrested."

"You have to question them!" I cry so sharply that Honey jumps up from where she was sleeping on my bed. "They may know where Mom is. There were marks in the dirt by the barn from cages and footprints—large men's shoes and a smaller one that looks like Mom's boots. Also, we found a fake pug pedigree certificate."

"Footprints and pedigree at that old barn?" Curiosity rises in his voice. "How do you know the pedigree isn't real?"

"Leo researched it and found fake information."

"I know Leo's clever, but Katherine would have notified me if she found evidence of a crime."

"Maybe she didn't get a chance." My legs suddenly feel weak, and I sink onto a chair.

"I find it hard to believe the Midgley brothers are responsible for your mother's absence. Burl and Merle are lazy and dishonest, but not dangerous. Still, I'll stop by their mother's house and talk to them. If Katherine is in danger, I won't rest until she's safe," he adds solemnly. "I promise."

Mom made a promise once too. And I know she would have kept it if she could.

I set the phone on my dresser and hear a soft mew. Honey springs onto the bed and curls up beside me, purring. I pet her silky orange fur and rest on a pillow. Suddenly I'm so exhausted I can't keep my eyes open...

Ding!

The sound startles me awake. I blink around an empty room. How long have I been sleeping?

There's another ding and a vibration from my pocket. Oh yeah, I still have my sisters' phone. I glance at a text from some guy named Raymond, shove the phone back into my pocket, and leave the room. The rest of the house is oddly quiet.

"Oh, you're awake." My grandmother's voice startles me, and I whirl around to find her peering from the kitchen doorway, a dishrag in her hands.

"Where are my sisters?" I gesture around the room.

"They went back to their friend's house. I told them I'd call if I heard anything."

She offers to make me a snack. I'm not interested in eating, but my stomach is rumbling so I follow her into the kitchen. I'm staring at a chicken salad sandwich, trying to make myself eat, when the doorbell rings. I'm sure who it is, so I push back my chair and race out of the kitchen.

"Becca! Leo!" I cry as I open the door. "I'm so glad you're here."

Leo hangs back, but Becca rushes forward with open arms and a hug. "Kelsey, have you heard anything?"

"Mom sent another text, but it didn't sound like her." I shiver. "I think someone made her send it. But everyone else thinks she's okay."

"You have to tell Sheriff Fischer what we've found out," Becca says.

"I did. I don't think he believes me, but he promised to investigate."

Leo is still standing on the porch, looking down at his feet and not meeting my gaze.

Shame rushes through me. "I'm sorry, Leo," I say softly. "I shouldn't have hung up on you."

"I agree, but it's okay," he says, shifting his feet awkwardly.

"Come on inside." I tug him into the house. His fingers curl around mine. Our eyes meet, and we both drop our hands.

"What can we do to help?" Becca asks.

"Being here helps," I say with a grateful look at them. "We'll keep looking for Mom. I feel sure now that she was tracking down the puppy mill crooks. The info Leo found about the pedigree proves puppies were being kept at the barn. Sheriff Fischer is going to investigate the Midgley brothers since they have a history of running puppy mills. But I have a different lead to follow." I glance into the kitchen where Gran Nola is emptying the dishwasher. If she knew what I was planning, she'd only worry. Worse, she might not let me leave the house.

"I need to get outside for a while. Let's take the dogs to the dog park," I say loud enough for my grandmother to hear. I ask her to call me on my sisters' cell if there's any news.

Handsome and Major bark excitedly, wagging their tails when we click on their leashes. Becca and I ride our bikes, while Leo rolls on his gyroboard, holding both dog leashes like a cart being pulled by a team of horses.

The dog park is a fenced-in area of the Valley Pine Park a few blocks from my grandmother's house. It doesn't take long to ride there. It's a quiet time of the day, between lunch and dinner, and only a few people are around. We sit on a bench in a shady corner away from the other dog walkers and watch our dogs romp across the grass.

"It's been hard waiting around for news when I'd rather be looking for Mom," I admit, a lump in my throat. "I kept thinking about Leo's suspicion that the barn was used for a puppy mill, so I researched online."

Becca leans in close. "What did you find out?"

"Puppy mills are bad news. Crowded cages, overbreeding, and diseases. Regular puppies usually sell for a few hundred dollars each, but with a fake pedigree claiming the pup is champion bred, the price could be as much as two thousand."

"Exactly," Leo says. "According to my calculations, one hundred pups at two thousand each equal two hundred thousand dollars."

"Wow!" Becca's dark eyes widen. "Buggy would probably have been sold with a fake pedigree if she hadn't gotten away. Those horrible breeders need to be stopped, or lots of people will be scammed."

"Like my sister's friend Delainey." I arch my brows dramatically. "She's buying a pug from someone she met online. The pug is supposed to be purebred with a champion lineage, yet it's selling for half-price. I called Delainey to find out more details."

Becca taps her mauve-painted fingernails on the bench. "What did she say?"

"Delainey found the breeder—Merry Lee Vandameer—through a pug discussion group. I checked out her website and it was really professional, not what I'd expect from puppy mill crooks. There were quotes from satisfied buyers and lots of photos of people with their puppies. And Mrs. Vandameer is flying all the way here from Tennessee to deliver the puppy."

"Any web designer can create an impressive page." Leo pulls up the Vandameer Premiere Pugs website on his phone. "I'll admit this looks professional, but appearances can be deceiving."

I glance over his shoulder as he scrolls through puppy photos. "That pug could be Buggy," I say, pointing.

"Except for the fact it's a male," Leo reads off the screen. "He was sired by a grand champion named Tiger Tumbler Chadwick."

"Tiger is a cute dog name," Becca says. "And look at this adorable pug." The pug's ears have pink bows, and she's wearing a tutu like a ballerina.

"Her trophy is bigger than she is." I smile. "Twice her size."

"Her name is big too...Duchess Delphina of Snowship Songs."

Leo squints down at the phone. "Hmm, I've seen that photo before with a different caption. The pup's name was Sandpiper Glowing Icicle."

"Are you sure?" Becca asks. "Pug puppies look so much alike."

"I have an exceptional memory for details. Notice how the right eyebrow is lifted but the left one isn't? And the pink tutu is crooked," he says as his fingers tap on the screen. "Also the pup's parents are the same, although from a different breeder."

"Could a dog have two names and two owners?" I turn to Becca.

"Not on the official certificate." Becca scrunches her nose in puzzlement. "One of the breeders is lying."

"The one offering a discount." Leo taps on his tablet, then looks up with a triumphant expression. "Merry Lee Vandameer from Tennessee is a phony. Except for the website—which is probably a complete fabrication—there is no information on her online."

"I knew it!" I snap my fingers. "She's as fake as the pedigree certification I found."

"So who's delivering a pug to your sister's friend?" Becca asks.

"The CCSC will find out tomorrow," I say as an idea forms. "We'll stake out Delainey's house and watch as the pug is delivered."

Leo nods, but Becca looks uneasy. "Shouldn't we tell Sheriff Fischer?"

"We don't know enough yet," I say. "We have multiple suspects—Mr. Barton and the Midgley brothers. But the sheriff thinks the puppy mill was shut down and that the Midgley brothers who ran it aren't dangerous. So we need solid proof."

"Like catching the criminals in an illegal transaction," Leo says excitedly. "We have sufficient time to organize a strategy using my drones for surveillance and GPF trackers. Frankie can help with disguises for the stakeout."

"Good idea," Becca approves. "After the pup is delivered, we'll track Mrs. Vandameer to the puppy mill."

"And to Mom," I say hopefully.

While the dogs run around the fenced-in park, we work out our plan. Leo will fly his bird drone over Delainey's house, and we'll study the video for a good surveillance location. Frankie will disguise us so we can spy undercover as Merry Lee Vandameer delivers Luna. We'll find a way to stick one of Leo's Global Positioning Finder (GPF) balls to her clothing or hair. When Merry Lee returns to the puppy mill, the GPF tracker will transmit her location to Leo's computer. Sheriff Fischer will shut down the puppy mill and arrest Mrs. Vandameer, and hopefully we'll find my mom. Case solved.

Clipping the leashes back on the dogs, we leave the park, eager to get started on our plan.

We're a block from my grandmother's house when my sisters' phone dings. It could be Gran Nola, so I slow my bike and pull over to the sidewalk. The short message shocks me like a stun gun.

"What's wrong?" Becca rolls up beside me on her bike. "Is it from your mother?"

"No, from Delainey. She doesn't know I still have Kenya's phone. She wants my sister to come over because the puppy delivery date has been changed."

"To when?" Leo asks, holding tight to the dogs' leashes.

"Today." I swallow hard. "In twenty minutes."

"Plan canceled." Leo holds the dogs' leashes tightly in one hand and makes a guillotine chop gesture with the other. "It would take fourteen minutes to ride to my house to gather our spy equipment, leaving only six minutes to reach Delainey's house."

"And we don't know where she lives," I add, discouraged.

"I vote we call Sheriff Fischer," Becca says as she reaches over her handlebars to pet the dogs. "He can be annoying, but he's good at his job. And he'll listen to me because he really likes Mom, and wants me to like him too."

Leo turns to me with a thoughtful expression. "What do you want to do, Kelsey?"

"Spy on Delainey's house, except I don't know

her address." I snap my fingers. "But my sister does! I'll call Kenya and find out."

Out of habit, I hold out my hand to Becca to borrow her phone. Then I realize the weight in my pocket is a phone...my sisters' phone. How can I call Kenya when I have her phone?

Drats. Is there anyone else I can call?

I search my sisters' address list, and right at the top is Delainey Bitzkie. I already have her number, and now I have her last name too. When I scroll further down, there's her address!

"Delainey lives at 1109 Peggy Lane," I quickly tell Leo. "I think it's near the high school."

Leo hands the dogs over to Becca and consults his phone. A map of Sun Flower flashes on his screen. "Peggy Lane is 1.8 miles away. Calculating speed and distance, we can be there in eleven minutes— before the transaction time. Let's go."

But Becca frowns and points to the dogs. "What about Handsome and Major? Shouldn't we take them home first? It'll be hard to go unnoticed with two large dogs."

"No time," I say as I hop on my bike. "Besides, walking dogs has worked for us before. It's a good cover."

"Not as good a cover as the disguises Frankie would have created for us. If only we'd been able to implement our plan," Leo says with a disappointed sigh. He slips his phone into his pocket and draws out a few sticky GPF balls. "These are the only devices I have with me."

While a GPF ball once helped me out of a bad situation, I'd rather have Leo's spy drones. My favorite is the dragon drone. It could fly into Delainey's house like a nearly invisible spy.

"Lead the way, Leo," Becca says. She hands one leash to me.

I balance on my bike, gripping Handsome's leash in one hand. The dogs should be tired after romping at the park, but they seem to be made of endless energy. Handsome tugs on my leash, pulling me to go faster. And I can tell Becca is having to work hard to control Major too. When we near a crosswalk where the light is red, Major speeds up instead of slowing down.

"Stop, Major," Becca commands. "Stop!"

Major tugs on the leash as if he didn't hear Becca.

Leo glances back with a flash of alarm. He spins on his gyro-board and commands firmly, "*Steh*."

Instantly Major stops.

"Oh, I forgot he only obeys German words." Becca pats the dog's brown head. The light turns to green, and we continue in our doggy parade.

Peggy Lane is a quiet street. The houses are spread apart with grassy front yards and trees that cast shadows, perfect for concealing spies. We slow to a stop in the shade of a tall fence and huddle to talk strategy.

"Delainey's house is the blue one with the hedge," Leo whispers.

"There's a car in the driveway but none in front of the house," I say. "So I don't think Merry Lee is here yet."

Becca squints into the distance. "Is that Delainey peeking out from the door?"

I follow her gaze just in time to see black hair and a blur of someone wearing red go back into the house.

"I don't know what Delainey looks like, but if she sees us staring at her house, she'll get suspicious," I warn. "We can't stand on the sidewalk much longer."

"We can walk the dogs to the end of the block, then come back," Becca suggests.

I nod. "And when we're across from Delainey's house again, we'll make up a reason to stop that doesn't look suspicious."

Becca points to the loopy purple laces on her purple sneakers. "We can pretend to tie our shoes."

"Or pick up dog poop," I say as I pull out the plastic bag I'd tucked in my pocket before we left my grandmother's house.

"Poop tactics." Becca giggles. "It could work."

"While you walk the canines, I'll skate around the street very subtly." Leo spins a wheelie in front of us. "When the puppy sellers show up, I'll take a photo of the car's license plate and the occupants."

After Leo whirls away in a fancy spin, Becca and I walk slowly, pausing to talk like we're two ordinary girls walking our dogs after a long day at school. We talk about school and friends in case the breeze carries our words. But our gazes keep sliding to the blue house in the middle of the block.

"Look!" Becca whispers, grabbing my arm. "The girl with the black hair is peeking out the door again!"

"Must be Delainey," I whisper back.

I bend over and pet Handsome while I covertly study the girl. She's taller than me (which isn't saying much) and wears gold heels, a flowing cherry-red skirt, and a lacy white blouse with gold hoop earrings like she's dressed up for a date.

A puppy date, I think wryly. I feel sorry for Delainey, though, and wish I could warn her that Mrs. Vandameer is probably a phony. But warning Delainey could ruin everything.

I glance at my watch. Four minutes till delivery.

"Let's walk to the end of the street, then turn around and come back," I say.

"We should call Sheriff Fischer and let him take over," Becca suggests again.

Determination burns in me, and I shake my head. "We'll call him—but not until we have proof."

We walk to the end of the block and back. When we're across from Delainey's house again, there's still no sign of a visitor.

A whooshing noise startles me, and I turn to see Leo rolling down the sidewalk. He tilts up on two wheels, then jumps high and springs back on his gyro-board. Anyone watching would think he's a typical show-off skater, but I know it's all a ruse and he's studying the blue house. Instead of passing us, he slows to a stop.

He glances around furtively. "Anything to report?"

"We had a fake conversation," Becca says.

I love spying, but surveillance is like having an itch I can't scratch. I want to take action, not ride around like a carefree kid who doesn't have a missing mother. I glance at my watch again. "It's almost puppy time. I'm done waiting," I tell my club mates. "I'm going in."

"In?" Becca blinks at me.

I point across the street. "Delainey's house."

Becca frowns. "You can't be serious!"

"Excellent strategy," Leo says, which surprises me. "But take these with you." He holds out two GPF balls. They look like something you'd get out of a gum ball machine. "I had planned to shoot these at the suspect to track her locations, but this is a better plan. All you need to do is toss a GPF on Mrs. Vandameer's clothes or hair."

"Easy peasy," I say, pocketing the GPF balls. I pass Handsome's leash over to Becca.

My heart thuds loudly, and I breathe in and out in the deep, calming way Gran Nola has taught me. I smooth back my tousled hair with my hand and stride up to the front door. Before I lose my courage, I press the doorbell.

Delainey opens it. She's pretty, with high cheekbones and a sweet smile. Her long dark lashes flutter in surprise as she looks at me. "But you're not—"

"You were expecting my sister or Mrs. Vandameer," I finish for her with an apologetic grin. "I'm Kelsey."

"Kenya's little sister." She nods but seems puzzled. "What are you doing here? Where's Kenya?"

"She loaned me her phone and I saw your text, but I don't know where she is so I couldn't give her your message. Since I'm dying to see your puppy, I came over instead. I hope you don't mind."

Delainey grins. "Not at all! I'm glad you're here. This change of plans happened so fast that my parents are still at work and I'm here alone. I'm glad to have someone with me to share this amazing moment. I can't wait to meet little Luna!"

"Me too!" I wear a smile like camouflage. Spies must blend in and never show their true feelings.

"Mrs. Vandameer will be here soon," Delainey goes on as she ushers me into her house. "When you meet her, you can ask about a pug for your friend."

Friend? Oh yeah, the fake-friend who wants to buy a pug. "My friend will be excited."

"And if she gets a pug too, our puppies can have play dates. What's her name?"

The most convincing lie is one that contains some

truth so I answer, "Becca. She really loves dogs." Before Delainey can ask anything else, I change the subject and point down the hallway. At the end, there's a bench covered in dog toys, a plush bed, a leash, puppy food, and a sparkling pink collar. "Are those for Luna?"

"Yes. Mom teases that I'm spoiling my puppy before I even have her. But I wanted to be ready for her. I also have this." She pulls out an envelope from her pocket and waves it. "Exactly two thousand dollars."

"Wow," I say, surprised. I've never seen that much money in cash.

She shrugs. "Merry Lee insisted on cash. She told me, 'You're buying a beloved family member, not a car.'"

I press my lips together, even more suspicious. Cash can't be traced.

"I hear a car!" Delainey squeals and rushes to the door. "My Luna is finally here! I can't wait to meet her!"

And I can't wait to meet the mysterious Merry Lee Vandameer.

I follow Delainey outside.

Chapter 19

Pursuit!

It's like the world has stopped in a freeze-frame. I take everything in with a sweeping glance. A middle-aged woman wearing a long, flowered skirt and a floppy sun hat steps out of an SUV with shaded windows. In the SUV, a shadowy figure sits waiting. Across the street, Becca and Leo wait— one pretending to check a tire on her bike and the other on his gyro-board.

Delainey rushes over to Mrs. Vandameer and scoops up a tiny black puppy. Luna is even smaller than Buggy, which hardly seems possible. Her bark is more of a squeak, and her curly tail wiggles excitedly.

"My little Luna," Delainey croons lovingly. When she finds out the pedigree papers are fake, she's going to be disappointed.

I go over to Delainey. "She's so cute," I say, petting Luna's velvety puppy fur.

Delainey gestures to me. "This is my friend Kelsey."

"It's a pleasure to meet y'all," the woman says. Her southern accent is so thick that I'm sure it's phony.

"Thank you for bringing Luna to me. She's the most darling puppy in the world!" Delainey kisses the puppy's black nose.

"I only care about finding the perfect home for my tiny treasures," Mrs. Vandameer says. "And it's obvious that this puppy was meant to be yours."

"She's adorable! It was so kind of you to make such a long trip to bring her to me. I've made some sweet tea and pecan cookies," Delainey adds graciously. "Please come inside, and your friend can come too." She points to the shadowed figure in the car.

"Thank you kindly, but he's just my driver. I always hire a car when I travel." Mrs. Vandameer waves her red-painted nails. "I'm on a tight schedule and need to hurry back to the airport. Sorry I can't stay, although tea and cookies sound delicious." She unclasps a briefcase and takes out a manila envelope. "Here are all of Luna's documents. I assume you have my payment in cash?"

"Right here," Delainey says and holds out the envelope.

I want to scream, "No! Don't give her the money!"

Instead I grasp a GPF ball and move closer to Mrs. Vandameer. I'm aware of the shadowy watcher in the car so I wait until her back is turned toward me, then fling the GPF ball.

And I miss.

Drats. I only have one more GPF.

"Are you sure you don't want to come inside?" Delainey asks, then giggles when the puppy licks her face.

"No. You've been kind enough," the woman says with a satisfied smile. She opens the envelope and counts the cash. "I have all I need."

But I don't, I think, grasping the GPF. When she turns to leave, I move beside her and touch her shoulder. "Wait a minute, Mrs. Vandameer. I have a question."

She pushes back a silvery strand of hair that curls so perfectly I suspect she's wearing a wig. "How can I help you, my dear?"

"A friend of mine would like a purebred pug. Delainey said you might consider giving her a discount."

"I certainly would." Her smile curves wide, and I can almost see dollar signs dancing in her eyes. "You just tell your friend to call me." She rattles off the same number Delainey gave me, and I nod like this is the first time I'm hearing it.

When Mrs. Vandameer turns to leave, I spot a shiny glint on the back of her jacket. I grin. Score one GPF ball!

She steps into her "hired" car and speaks to the driver—a thirtysomething man with a dark-blond beard and camo cap. I can't hear what she says, but she calls him Burl.

Burl? As in the puppy mill crooks Burl and Merle Midgley? A wild thought hits me. Could Merry Lee Vandameer be their mother?

The SUV engine rumbles as the car backs out of the driveway.

I turn around. "I have to go!" I tell Delainey. "I just remembered an appointment I'm late for."

"But you haven't even held Luna, and I have cookies and sweet tea. Stay just a little longer."

Across the street, my club mates gesture for me to hurry.

"Sorry, but this is important," I say, rushing down the porch steps. "Luna really is sweet. I'm happy for you."

But I'm worried too. What will happen to Luna when the puppy mill crooks are caught? Will Delainey have to give up her puppy? Could justice be crueler than the crime?

"Hurry!" Becca says as I hop on my bike.

Leo rolls up beside me. His phone's screen shows a map with a blue dot moving across it.

"Good job placing the GPF," Leo says. "But we have to move quickly. They're already turning the corner."

How can Leo expect two bikes and a gyro-board to catch up with a car? As long as the car stays on residential streets, we have a chance. But if they head for the airport, we'll lose them. Leo leads the way, crouching low as he gains speed, and I sail around the corner behind my friends.

We pass the high school, where only a few kids and teachers are around this late in the afternoon.

We're a block behind our target, but we should be able to catch up at the stop sign ahead. Except that the SUV doesn't slow; it runs the stop sign.

"Go faster!" Leo shouts, then shoots off ahead of us.

"I can't go any faster," Becca tells me. "Besides, Major is getting tired."

"Handsome too." He's panting hard, and I slow down. Chasing after bad guys with dogs is a bad idea.

"The dogs need a rest and water," Becca says, rolling up beside me. "I think we should text the sheriff."

"Yeah, go ahead," I say. "But if we stop, we'll lose Leo."

"You catch up with Leo, and I'll take both dogs," she says, holding out her hand for Handsome's leash. "I'll text to find out where you are. Do you still have your sisters' phone?"

I nod, glancing down the street. I can barely see Leo, who has zoomed ahead on his robotic board.

"After the dogs are rested, I'll find you," Becca says, tucking both leashes into one hand.

"Okay." I look ahead just as Leo makes a right and disappears around a corner. I wave to Becca.

"Got to go!"

I pedal away, following Leo onto Main Street, which leads into downtown. Usually red lights are annoying, but right now I'm thrilled to see a traffic jam. When Leo stops on the sidewalk a few cars behind the SUV, I finally catch up with him.

I bend over to look at the map on Leo's phone. The flashing dot has momentarily stopped. "Where do you think they're headed?"

"According to my calculations, there are two likely routes," Leo says. "If they go straight, they'll be in a busy neighborhood with lots of stop signs, which will make them easier to follow. But if they turn left, they'll leave town."

"Mrs. Vandameer said she was going to the airport," I tell him.

"If she's being honest, then we're out of luck. My GPF range is only five miles. But I've taken photos and have the license plate memorized." He glances around curiously. "Where are Becca and the dogs?"

I explain quickly before the light turns green.

As we near the next intersection, I hold my breath. *Don't turn left. Go straight*! I cross my fingers. And the SUV turns right.

Drats! That's not even a street!

"Down the alley!" Leo shouts as he skids around the corner.

I follow, dodging around broken glass and trash until we reach a quiet country road.

"Where did they go?" I shade my eyes from the glinting sun as I stare down the narrow road bordered with orchards of fruits and nut trees.

"Of all the confounded complications," Leo utters in what I guess is the closest he comes to swearing. "The GPF indicator went out."

"It's not working?" I look at his phone for the flashing dot and only see a blank gray screen.

"Signal is lost and...It's returned! But that's odd." He wrinkles his brow. "How can the car be on the other side of Sun River? The map doesn't show a bridge."

"Maybe the car floated down the river," I joke.

"Not that model of vehicle. Although Tesla has a car with a wheel rotation that can propel the car through a body of water without damaging the battery." Leo shakes his blond head. "There has to be a bridge. If we keep going on this road, we should find it."

I pause to send a quick text to Becca, then pedal

fast to catch up with Leo. The road becomes hilly, sweeping up, then down like I'm riding a roller coaster. A wind picks up, whooshing my hair behind me.

The road curves to the left and abruptly ends at a bramble of berry bushes that sweep down to Sun River.

"The app shows we need to be on the other side of the river." Leo points. "But no bridge."

"Don't even think about asking me to swim," I say with a shiver. Sun River looks inviting with rippling waves sparkling like diamonds, but it's actually freezing with treacherous undercurrents.

"We must have missed the turn." Leo frowns. "Let's go back."

I nod and turn my bike around. We ride slowly, peering in through bushes and trees for a road. But there isn't any. We've gone halfway when I notice a faded square of wood nailed to a sprawling oak tree. A street sign? I pull my bike off the road and try to read the faint writing.

"'Down the…something…hole…Bob'?" I murmur.

"Down the rabbit hole," Leo says as he comes up behind me.

"But what does it mean? And who is Bob?"

"Look!" Leo gestures to a tangle of fruit trees. "A dirt road!"

"With fresh tire tracks." I point. "This must be where Mrs. Vandameer's driver turned off."

Leo's screen shows we're closing in on the flashing dot. We decide it's safer to continue by foot so we hide my bike and his gyro-board in the bushes.

Trees drape over us like thick curtains blocking out the sun. The road rises, dips, and plunges toward Sun River. Tire ruts deepen, crisscrossing with different treads as if several vehicles have come this way recently. When the trees open to a clearing with a wooden covered bridge, I gasp. "There *is* a bridge."

Leo snaps his fingers. "I knew there had to be a logical explanation for how the SUV crossed the river. And look up ahead—a roof."

I lift my gaze. "Is that a rabbit weather vane on top?"

Leo nods. "Animal designs are the most common for weather vanes. The most famous weather vane is the grasshopper atop Faneuil Hall in Boston. Weather vanes were historically useful because approaching weather systems could be anticipated by the direction of the wind."

"It's easier to check a weather app," I say with a shrug as I take out my sisters' phone.

After texting Becca with directions, I catch up with Leo as he enters the covered bridge. I'm enveloped in darkness and the smell of damp wood. Shivering, I wrap my arms around my shoulders until I come out into the light on the other side. Tire tracks lead to a faded white picket gate that hangs open. A sign reads: Down the Rabbit Hole, Bed-and-Breakfast Inn.

Below the sign, a word is scrawled in large black letters: CLOSED.

Not *Bob*, I realize, but *B and B*. But if it's closed, why is the gate wide open?

"Impressive architecture." Leo lifts his gaze to a charming Victorian with gables, turrets, and fancy trim around the windows.

"It seems lonely," I murmur.

There's an air of abandonment, like the place is under an enchantment and has been sleeping for many years. Grime-covered windows are like sleepy eyes shutting out the world, while rampant weeds strangle the lawn and garden. The only clues that someone lives here are the open gate, the SUV parked beside a garage, and the barking. High-pitched yapping sounds like those of dozens of little dogs. And it's coming from the garage.

I've found the puppy mill!

Finally, I have proof for the sheriff. I hope he's gotten Becca's text and is on the way.

I turn excitedly to Leo—only he's not there. Putting my hands on my hips, I look around but don't see him. There's a rustle from the brambly bushes behind a metal shed.

"Leo?" I whisper nervously.

I step forward just as a tiny rabbit bursts out of the bushes and vanishes into the weeds. I jump back, startled, then smile at my fears. It's just a wild rabbit.

But where is Leo? I scan the overgrown foliage. He can't be in the shed because it's padlocked. Maybe behind it? I walk around the shed and find him pulling branches from dense bushes.

"What are you doing?" I ask, my hands on my hips.

He looks at me with a strange expression. Saying nothing, he pulls back a large leafy branch and points into the bushes.

I gasp at a dirty white vehicle.

My mother's truck.

Chapter 20

Down the Rabbit Hole

My mind races as I stare at the truck. How long has it been here? Who covered it up with branches? And most importantly, where is my mother?

"No one's inside." Leo gestures to the truck as if he's guessed my fear.

"She's here somewhere," I say in a small, scared voice.

Leo points to the B and B. "The most logical location would be in the house."

"Or the garage where I heard dogs barking." I shudder as I think of the large cage imprint I found on the barn floor. "I'm going to look for her."

Leo shakes his head. "No. We should wait here for the sheriff. I don't want anything to happen to you."

"But she might be scared and hurt! We can't wait... What's that noise?" I swivel toward the rustling trees bordering the road. "Someone's coming!"

"It's probably another wild rabbit," Leo suggests with a shrug.

"Whatever it is, it's coming closer!" I gape wild-eyed as I hear a low whirring sound like wheels. "We have to hide."

Before I can move, two dogs and a grinning girl burst from the trees.

"Finally, I found you!" Becca cries as she's half dragged by the dogs. Her leopard bandanna sags, and her usually glittery sneakers are caked with dirt. But she looks wonderful to me.

"Becca!" I rush to meet her.

"I had a terrible time getting here." She pushes back her hair and adjusts her bandanna. "I hit a pothole, and now my tire is flat. It's a miracle I made it."

I squeeze her hand. "I'm so glad you found us."

"I was really lost until Major barked at the road," she says, wiping dirt from her arm. "What is this place anyway?"

"A closed B and B that may be a puppy mill." I gesture at the garage, then lead her over to the shed and pull aside the bushes. "Look what Leo found."

"OMG!" Becca's hands fly to her face. "Is that what I think it is?"

"My mother's truck." Fear twists my gut. "We have to find her."

Leo shakes his head. "It's too dangerous to go near the house."

"He's right. If there are bad guys here, we don't want to mess with them." Becca hands me the leashes to hold and whips out her phone. "We need the sheriff. He hasn't answered my texts so I'll try calling him directly."

"The last time I tried to call him, I got his snotty deputy."

"But I know his private number," Becca says with a wry smile. "It's a perk of him dating Mom."

While Becca calls, I shift my feet impatiently. I pluck a leaf from the bush and slowly rip it into pieces.

"Sheriff Fischer, it's Becca." She gives me a "told you so" look, then adds dramatically, "We've found Mrs. Case's truck!"

Leaf pieces fall from my hand as I lean forward to listen.

"Kelsey recognized it." Becca nods at something the sheriff says. "Yeah, she's here with me, and Leo too...uh-huh...at the Down the Rabbit Hole bed-and-breakfast inn. I know it's closed, but we think it's being used as a puppy mill...What? You can't be serious. Okay, bye." She purses her peach-frosted lips as she clicks off.

"Is Sheriff Fischer on his way?" Leo asks.

"He'll come as soon as he can get away from the scene of a car accident. I heard sirens in the background." She scowls. "And he ordered us to leave."

"Not without Mom," I say stubbornly, wiping my leaf-stained hands on my jeans. "I know she's here somewhere. Maybe the garage."

Leo puts a calming hand on my arm. "Kelsey, you can't rush in there. They could have weapons or attack dogs."

"We have a trained former police dog," I point out.

"Major is tired." Becca pats the German shepherd on his head. "I'm worried about your mother too, but Sheriff Fischer told us to leave because he wants us to be safe. We should let him do his job."

"I'm not going until I see what's in that garage," I insist. "I'll be careful and stay out of sight."

Before they can stop me, I run across the weedy ground and through the open gate. They call my name, but I ignore them. I run fast, staying low. The house looks dark, but light shines from the garage windows. The Midgleys must be inside, and Mom could be there too. I'm not going to do anything stupid like try to rescue Mom alone. I just want to see my mother...to make sure she's okay.

As I slink across the weedy lawn, the sinking sun casts deep shadows that make me feel invisible.

Ducking behind the SUV, I check that the coast is clear. Then I creep closer to the garage, a square wood-sided building separate from the house. The large metal door is rolled closed, but there's a side door and several windows. Barking echoes from within the building. Creeping to a window, I hold my breath and peer through the glass.

Cages. Dozens of them! All full of tiny bug-eyed pugs. Mostly puppies, but there are a few older dogs too. I try to see farther into the room, but stacked cages block my view. I tiptoe around to the window on the other side.

I gasp. Burl Midgley is lifting a puppy from a cage. We're inches apart—only separated by the glass pane. His head turns in my direction, and I duck down. My heart thuds like crazy. I've stopped breathing. Silently I count to one hundred, blow out a shaky breath, and rise back to the window.

Burl is gently petting a puppy as he listens to Mrs. Vandameer talk. There's also a shorter man who resembles Burl and has a scraggly dark beard that dangles to his chest—his brother Merle, I'm sure.

But no sign of Mom.

Could she be inside the B and B house? I look up, up where the rabbit weather vane meets the sky. There must be dozens of rooms in that huge house. I can't stay here much longer, but I can't give up without checking the B and B. It should be safe, since the Midgleys are in the garage.

The front door is unlocked. When I step inside, the wooden floor creaks loudly. I sweep my gaze around to look for any sign of danger, but the house is quiet. I move cautiously through the foyer into a high-ceilinged living room where cloths gray with dust drape over the furniture. I lift a cloth to find a velvety gold-colored couch underneath. I notice dusty footprints on the floor. A large print has the same wavy grooves as the ones we found by the abandoned barn.

I follow the footprints past a winding staircase and down a narrow hall decorated with gilt-framed portraits of presidents. I got an A on a quiz on presidents so I recognize Lincoln, Washington, and Jackson. My teacher would be proud, I think with a wry smile.

The footprints stop at a heavy wooden door with an old-fashioned copper knob. I press my ear against the wood, listening. No sounds. I grasp the knob and cautiously twist. The door swings open. I stare into a room with a gigantic desk as a centerpiece and empty shelves bordering the walls. Unlike the other rooms, this floor looks as if it's been cleaned recently. And the desk has a pen, a stapler, a tissue box, a computer, a printer, and a pile of papers.

I cross over to the desk, smelling a fresh-off-the-printer odor. I reach for a paper, then pull back because I don't want to leave my fingerprints. Plucking a tissue from the box on the desk, I use it to pick up another certified pedigree like the one I found in the barn. A whole stack of the forged pedigrees!

My pocket dings. I keep forgetting I'm carrying my sisters' phone. Luckily, it didn't ding while I was spying at the garage, or the Midgleys would have found me.

The text is from Becca in big, bold letters:

Get out! Now! Danger!

Panic surges through me. I shove the phone back into my pocket and run across the room. As I reach for the door, a sharp creak echoes through the house. Someone has stepped on that squeaky foyer floor.

There's no running away—danger is here!

Footsteps click-clack down the hall toward me.

Hide! my mind screams. But there's nothing in the room except the huge desk. I yank the desk chair back and cram myself into the small space. For once, I'm glad to be short.

"Of all the fool things," a woman says as high heels click into the room. Although there's no phoney-baloney southern twang, I recognize Mrs. Vandameer's voice.

I hug my arms around my knees and try not to breathe.

"I ask my boys to do one simple thing, and those imbeciles can't do it," she mutters. Papers rustle over my head. Please don't come around the desk, I think desperately.

I shift, trying to get comfortable. It's cramped and dusty. Whoever cleaned the room didn't go under the desk. A cough tickles in my throat, and I cover my mouth. *Do not cough*!

Footsteps pound from outside the room, and a man says, "Mom, will you hurry? Merle and I don't know where you want the older dogs. Shouldn't the moms go with their pups?"

"No. Only the pups are going," she snaps in an irritated tone. "I told you and your idiot brother that at least a dozen times. Do whatever you want with the older dogs. Leave them or kill them. I don't care."

"I don't like hurting animals," he argues. "Can't we sell them too?"

"Not for enough," she says roughly. "Adult dogs barely sell for a few hundred—and even less if they're sick. We're scoring a thousand per puppy from the pet store distributor, and I've made twice that for the pups I sold on the side."

Burl gives a low whistle. "Too bad that one pup got away from us at the barn. Should we go and look again?"

"Don't be stupid," his mother snaps. "We can't stick around here anymore. The sheriff stopped by our house this morning asking about you boys."

"Don't let him arrest us," Burl whines like a scared little boy. "Jail food sucks."

"I didn't tell him anything," she assures him, then slips into a southern accent. "I'm just a sweet old lady trying her best to care for her sons. We'll be out of here as soon as the pups are picked up."

"Then will you let the lady go?" Burl adds in a worried tone. "No one knows she's here and she didn't see our faces, so she can't get us in trouble. You said you'd let her out when we left."

"She's fine where she is." Her cold voice chills me, because I'm sure they're talking about Mom.

Mom *is* here somewhere. She's okay…for now.

But I'm in big trouble if I'm caught. I feel the weight in my pocket from the phone. If someone dings with a text, the Midgleys will know I'm here! Quickly, I switch the phone to silent.

"Leave the worries to me, Burl," his mother adds in a softer tone. "After today, we're done with puppy mills. We'll have enough money to finally get out of this boring little town. We can travel anywhere in the world we want."

"Merle and I were talking about that," Burl says cautiously. "We know where we want to go."

"Where?" Her tone sharpens like pointy knives.

"Disneyland. We ain't been there in a while. I like the pirate ride."

"Seriously, grow up!" I hear a sharp slap. "You're thirty-four years old—not four! Get back in the garage and prepare the pups for travel. The transport truck will be here soon."

"Whatever you say, Mom." He shuffles away, the door thudding shut.

Mrs. Midgley swears under her breath again about her "idiot sons." My mother would *never* say mean things about her kids. I almost feel sorry for the Midgley brothers. But I'm more worried about Mom and scared for myself. One of my legs is going numb. And the cough in my throat itches to come out. Leave already! I want to scream.

But the mean mother continues to shuffle through papers.

"All the certificates are here," she murmurs. "But where did I put the lockbox key?"

I hear rummaging noises like she's searching a purse. Keys jingle and she says, "Here it is!"

High heels click on the wooden floor toward the desk where I'm hiding. If she notices the chair is sticking out, she may look down and see me.

Heels click-clack closer.

She reaches out with long, bony fingers toward my hiding place...

- Chapter 21 -
Moving Day

The chair is shoved forward—smashing into me.

Ouch! Instead of screaming, I grit my teeth. I flatten myself and pretend I'm part of the desk.

Don't look down, I think desperately as she draws close.

"Stupid chair," she says as she reaches for a bottom desk drawer. She's so close she could reach out and slap me.

While I can't see much from my squished position, I hear the metallic click of a key inserted in a lock, followed by a drawer sliding open. She must be taking out the lockbox she mentioned. Hinges creak and paper shuffles. Then Mrs. Midgley turns away, heels click-clacking out of the room.

Whew! Close call!

I unpretzel myself from beneath the desk, but when I try to stand, I almost fall over. My leg has gone numb. I rub my leg muscles, then move toward the door...until I remember the lockbox. What's inside? I stare at the box as if superglue is sticking me to the floor.

My mystery novels warn that it's a bad idea to mess with a crime scene. Leave the evidence for the authorities. But I decide to take just a quick peek and pluck out a tissue to cover my fingerprints.

The lockbox isn't locked. Inside are receipts, envelopes, and a stack of cash with a hundred-dollar bill on top. Thousands of dollars! I don't care about the cash, but I recognize writing on one envelope and shove it in my pocket. Whirling around, I scurry like a scared rabbit out of the house.

Ducking behind a porch rail, I glance around to make sure the coast is clear. Shadows move through the window, and the barking grows louder. But no one is outside. I sprint across the lawn, through the open gate, and around the shed where my friends jump up to meet me.

"Kelsey!" Becca throws her arms around my shoulders. "I was so worried—especially when that

woman and the bearded dude went into the house.
I tried texting, but you didn't answer."

"I shut off the phone because I was hiding under
a desk."

"OMG! I'm so glad you didn't get caught," Becca
cries.

Leo frowns. "You shouldn't have gone in there."

"I had to look for Mom. But it was scary." I
shudder. "I would have been caught if Becca hadn't
texted me."

"Leo started to go after you," Becca says with a
fond look at Leo. "But I held him back. Fortunately,
you're okay and help will be here soon. The sheriff
texted that he's on his way."

"He better hurry. The horrible woman said she
was leaving Mom where she is!" I throw up my
hands. "Wherever that is!"

"The sheriff will find her." Becca gives a start
and points at the road. "I think he's coming now! I
hear a car!"

"Yes!" I pump my arm in the air.

We don't want Sheriff Fischer to know we didn't
leave like he told us to, so we duck out of sight
behind the shed and watch the road.

The ground rumbles and branches quiver. The

engine sounds noisier and larger than the sheriff's pickup truck. When a large, gray moving truck rumbles out of the grove of trees, I gasp.

Not the sheriff, but the puppy movers!

"No! They can't be here already!" I cry with a panicked look at my friends. "They're going to take all the puppies away. They'll probably sell them to pet stores. And the Midgleys will abandon or kill the older dogs!"

"I'm texting the sheriff again," Becca says, tapping on her phone. "I told him to hurry!"

We huddle together in the shadows by the small shed, staring across the driveway as the large, gray truck backs up by the garage. I wrap my arms around Handsome and tell him to stay quiet. Major whines softly and sniffs the air as if he's poised for action.

I try not to panic and to focus on details to tell the sheriff. The truck is gray with no distinctive writing on the sides, and it has a California license plate. The truck's cab is black with tinted windows, but the driver's window is rolled down and I glimpse a black-haired woman wearing a sports cap and denim overalls.

Burl and Merle Midgley step out of the garage. "Over here!" Burl waves to the driver.

Mrs. Midgley joins them. She gestures for her sons to go into the garage and talks to the driver as the rear of the truck is lowered. Mrs. Midgley is giving orders, clearly in charge. Her bearded sons ping-pong back and forth, lugging cages of puppies from the garage to the truck. They carry a few closed crates too. One crate is so large that both men carry it together.

I stare at that crate. It's big enough to hold a person.

OMG! Could Mom be imprisoned inside?

Beside me, Handsome whines. "Shush," I whisper as he shifts anxiously beside me.

"They're closing the back of the truck," Becca cries softly.

"What if Mom is in the large crate?" I bite my lip. "We have to stop them from leaving!"

"I'll puncture the tires." Leo holds out his key spider. "This is the 4.5 improved key spider. I brought it along in case we had a situation like this. I've added a screwdriver that is sharp enough to flatten a tire."

When he starts to rise, I tug him down. "Don't be crazy!" I say. "They'll catch you, and you don't want to mess with those bearded dudes."

"If only Sheriff Fischer would get here!" Becca spreads her arms in frustration, then turns to look back at the road.

"Why doesn't he hurry?" I ask, feeling scared. I hug Handsome so tightly that he squirms away from me.

"Nothing we can do except wait." Leo sighs. "I've memorized the license plate and snapped photo evidence for the sheriff."

The truck driver flips the latches shut on the back of the truck. She walks around to the cab and climbs in. I watch in horror as the door closes behind her. The engine revs up, diesel smoke puffing from the exhaust. The truck slowly rolls away from the garage.

I'm so desperate that I don't realize I'm no longer holding Handsome's leash until I hear Leo shout, "Not another rabbit!" at the same time Becca cries, "No, Handsome! Come back here!"

Handsome lunges across the weeds after the rabbit. I jump up to chase after him.

"Hey!" Burl Midgley hollers. "There's a dog and some kids!"

"What are you kids doing there?" Merle Midgley shouts.

His mother points at me. "I've seen that girl before!"

Burl Midgley starts to come after us, but his mother calls him back.

"Forget the kids, and get in the car!" she yells, gesturing to the SUV.

While Handsome disappears into high weeds after the rabbit, the Midgleys hop into the SUV. Doors slam. Dust flies as the SUV roars after the moving van.

I run after it, choking on dust. "No! Come back!"

But the Midgleys, the moving truck, and my hope of finding Mom are gone.

- Chapter 22 -
A Major Miracle

"Mom," I cry as I sink onto the ground.

Leo comes up beside me and takes my hand. "If your mother is in that truck, the sheriff will find her. But she may not be there. She could be locked in a room in the house."

Hope rushes through me. I only checked downstairs, not any of the upstairs rooms. Maybe Mom *is* there.

I run across the lawn, and Leo catches up with me. "Becca has Major and is looking for Handsome. I'll help you look for your mother," he says, jogging beside me.

We burst through the open gate, then dodge around the overgrown garden. We cut across a large square of pavement that must have been a basketball court once, though all that's left is a rusty metal pole. I hear a shrill noise and pause to listen. A siren wails, coming closer.

"The sheriff is here," Leo says, running up the steps of the porch. He turns back to the road and points at the official truck rolling up to the gate.

"Too late," I say with a sigh.

"He won't allow us to search the house," Leo says hurriedly. "But he's not here to stop us. Come on!"

I give Leo a grateful look as he takes my hand, and we enter the B and B house together.

The foyer floor squeaks as we step inside. Instead of going down to the office, we race upstairs. There isn't much time, so we split up. I search the second floor while Leo continues to the third. I yank open doors and look inside while calling out "Mom" until my throat hurts. There are three suites on this floor, each complete with kitchenettes and private bathrooms. I check closets, beneath dusty beds, and even bathtubs. But the only living things are spiders.

And when I meet Leo back on the second-floor landing, he shakes his head sadly. "Sorry," he says.

We head outside. Becca is holding Major's leash

while she talks to the sheriff. I glance over at the garage just as Deputy Phil enters it. What if Mom is still in there? But when the deputy comes out empty-handed a few minutes later, my shoulders sag. Mom is still missing.

And apparently Handsome is too, I find out when I talk to Becca.

"I started to look for him," Becca says apologetically as Major tugs on the leash. "But Sheriff Fischer wanted to talk to me, and I had to fill him in on everything."

The sheriff comes up and pats my shoulders sympathetically. "Becca says you overheard Mrs. Midgley say your mother is here."

I nod. "Yeah. Her son Burl asked if he could let Mom out, but his mother said Mom should stay where she was."

"Where?" the sheriff asks.

"I wish I knew," I say, my throat tightening. "I thought maybe the house or the garage, but we couldn't find her. And the brothers carried a large crate to the moving truck. I'm afraid Mom might have been inside."

"I memorized the license plate," Leo pipes up, then rattles it off.

Sheriff Fischer jots it down. "We'll find your mom soon. I'll admit, I didn't want you kids to get involved, but you've done a good job. You need to go home now. I'll contact you when there's news."

The sheriff goes over to his truck, and I turn to my friends. "I'm not going anywhere until we find Mom."

"We need to find Handsome anyway," Leo points out.

"I think I hear him barking behind the B and B." Becca touches her animal-print bandanna and tilts her head. "Let's go!"

"Wait," Leo says, an odd look on his face. He turns to point at the shed. "We haven't looked there."

I follow his gaze to the rusty metal shed. We've been hiding behind it, but I never really *looked* at it. But if Mom was inside, wouldn't she have made some noise? The shed isn't very big and leans to one side. It's rusted like it's decades old, but there's a newish metal lock on the door.

Leo takes his key spider from his pocket. He tries different keys until there's a ping and the lock falls off. I hold my breath as Leo grabs the sliding door and it creaks open...

Bulky shadows take shape in dark shed. A lawn

mower, a ladder, coiled hoses, a broom, a rake, and a weed-eater.

But no Mom.

"It was worth a try," Leo says sadly.

"The sheriff will find her," Becca says, forcing a cheerful tone. "Let's find Handsome and get out of here."

We split up, looking for Handsome. We call his name over and over, but he doesn't come. We meet up at the back of the house where it borders the river.

"He has to be here somewhere," I say, wiping sweat from my face.

"Could he be down there?" Becca points down the embankment where wild berry bushes tangle in a sharp drop down to the river.

"He could have chased a rabbit down a trail." I frown. "It won't be easy to find him."

"We have a tracking canine, so I suggest we use his skills," Leo says.

Becca and I share a "why didn't we think of that?" look. She unclips Major's leash and Leo commands, "*Such.*"

Although Major isn't wearing his working vest, the command works. He goes taut, sniffs the air, and presses his nose close to the ground.

And he's off like a sprung arrow!

Instead of going toward the berry bushes, he races through high grass to the front of the house, pounding through the weedy garden and up to the porch. After sniffing around the porch steps, he spins around and returns to the weedy garden. Sniffing, he continues to the paved basketball court, stops abruptly, and barks.

"Handsome isn't here," Becca tells the German shepherd. "Keep looking."

Major barks and paws at the cement.

"It's just an old court," I tell the dog.

Leo rubs his chin thoughtfully. "I don't think so."

"What do you mean?" I ask, surprised. "What else could it be?"

Leo paces the cement slab, stopping at a corner where weeds rise higher than Major. Leo bends over and grabs something metal. "Look at this!"

"What?" Becca and I peer down.

Beneath the weeds, metal glints. Leo drops to his knees and yanks weeds aside to reveal a heavy steel circle, like a manhole cover. And it's bolted shut with a heavy padlock. Leo taps on the metal cover...and someone taps back!

"Listen!" Leo shouts.

"Someone is under there!" Becca kneels, pushing back her hair as it swishes across her eyes.

"Mom!" I drop to the ground. I hear three short taps and three long taps.

"Morse code!" I cry, my hands flying to my face as I think back to my code books. I count the taps. "SOS!"

Leo pulls out his key spider and tries putting different keys into the lock. He groans and shakes his head. "This is a tough lock," he murmurs. "None of my keys are working."

"Clever gadget," the sheriff says as he comes up behind us. "But this may work better." He holds a heavy-duty bolt cutter.

Stepping back, I hold my breath as he wields the cutter and snaps off the lock.

The sheriff tugs on the metal hatch. It doesn't budge, so he grabs with both hands and yanks. There's a sharp creak.

The latch flips back, revealing a dark hole.

And my mother.

- Chapter 23 -
Truth, Lies, and Spies

Everything's crazy after that. Hugs, tears, and explanations.

Sheriff Fischer offers Mom water and leads her over to his truck. After she's sitting on a cushioned seat with a blanket draped over her shoulders, she apologizes. "I should have called for backup."

"Yes, you should have," he says in a stern tone but with a gentle expression. "Can you tell us what happened?"

"It was all so fast," she says with an exhausted sigh. "When Kelsey told me where she found Buggy—the pug pup—I recognized the barn. I went there after I left the animal shelter. I was just going to look around, but as I was turning on the road, I saw a car driving away from the barn, which made me suspicious. I followed it to the B and B and hid my truck. I was about to call for backup, but I heard barking from the garage. When I went to check it out, someone came up behind me and threw a bag over my head. I was lifted up and shoved down into a dark prison." Her voice croaks, and she gulps water. "He left me there."

She goes on to explain how she screamed and pounded against the hatch for hours. But no one came, so she felt around until she found a lamp. She was surprised to find that her "prison" was a bomb shelter with shelves and sealed containers of bottled water and packages of survival food. Luckily, the previous owners of the B and B kept it well stocked.

"No one knew where I was, and my purse and phone were in my truck," she continues wearily. "All I could do was wait to be rescued. At least my prison was comfortable. It has a living room, kitchenette, bunk beds, a port-a-potty, a lantern, and a bookcase full of books. Finally, I had some time for reading," she teases, but her voice is raspy as if she's spent days shouting for help.

She holds me close while she answers questions from the sheriff. Mom sounds calm and brave, but when we're tucked safely in the sheriff's car heading for home, she admits that she was scared no one would ever find her. "And I felt terrible for not picking you up at school," she adds. "You must have thought I'd forgotten you. But I'd never do that."

"I know," I say softly.

Mom smiles weakly. "I owe you a girls' day out."

"I'm just glad you're safe," I say and hug her again.

Mom's return becomes a family party at Gran Nola's house. Kyle brings pizza, and my grandmother dishes out strawberry ice cream. Lots of laughter and hugs, and all night long Dad holds tight to Mom's hand and looks at her like she's a miracle. No worries about divorce with my parents!

As I'm cleaning up dishes with my sisters, I take Kenya aside.

"I have something to give you." I wipe my damp hands on a towel, then withdraw a thick folded envelope from my pocket.

"For me?" She wipes soap from her chin.

"Actually, it belongs to your friend Delainey." I hand her the envelope. "It's the money she paid for Luna. Tell her the pedigree certificate is a fake, so she deserves her money back."

"Will she have to give up Luna?" my sister asks uneasily.

"I don't think so. There'll be so many pugs needing homes that no one will bother with a pup that already has one. At least I hope not," I say.

Gran Nola's phone rings.

It's the sheriff with great news: the Midgleys are in custody! They may have avoided jail before for running a puppy mill, but they won't be able to escape kidnapping charges.

Things are crazy for a few days. Of course, that doesn't mean I can stay home from school. Now that Mom's back, she's strict about not missing school unless I'm dying.

Between catching up on homework and answering all kinds of questions from classmates, the CCSC doesn't have time for a meeting or to look for lost pets. And when we talk at school, our topic is the Spring Fling dance.

Guess who decided to go?

I'm still not sure about the whole Leo-and-me thing, but Mom insisted on buying me the most beautiful shimmering lavender dress ever and matching strappy shoes with heels that make me three inches taller. How could I resist?

By Friday evening, only hours before the dance, I'm a nervous wreck. Becca is supposed to be here to help fix my hair and makeup. Leo and Trevor, Becca's date, will meet us later. Dad offered to be our chauffeur to the dance. I can hardly believe I'm going to a dance, but it's not like I'm going on a real date. Leo and I are just friends.

While I stand helplessly in front of the mirror, trying different hairstyles, my grandmother comes to stand beside me. "Need any help?" she offers.

"Becca will be here soon to fix my makeup," I say, then notice her sad expression. "But you can help with my hair."

Gran smiles—a first since Greta picked up Major yesterday. I know she's glad Greta is well enough to take her dog home, but we all miss Major.

"Your hair would look nice up like this," my

grandmother says. She takes the brush and strokes my hair, twists it, and clips it up.

I stare into the mirror. "Wow, I look so much older...like I'm in high school."

"Maybe you should wear it down," she says with a chuckle. "I'm not ready for you to be that old yet."

I like the mature look, though, and keep my hair up. Minutes later, the doorbell rings. Finally, Becca is here to help with my makeup!

Becca looks beautiful in an ivory chiffon dress with a sequined olive jacket—and she's not alone.

"You brought Buggy." I reach out for the pug, and she licks my fingers. "But dogs can't go to dances."

"Why not? She can dance on her back legs," Becca jokes. "But seriously, I didn't bring her for us." Becca walks past me and over to my grandmother. She holds out the puppy. "Buggy needs a home, and your home needs a puppy."

My grandmother's eyes widen, and for a moment I'm afraid she's going to refuse. But then she grins. "You're right. Major is gone, and Handsome probably won't be here much longer. My home does need a puppy...and so do I. Thank you, Becca."

Gran Nola takes Buggy into her arms, crooning,

"What a sweet little girl. And your eyes really do bug out."

She's cradling Buggy like a baby as I tug on Becca's hand. We go down the hall and into the bathroom where makeup bottles and tubes scatter across the countertop.

"Becca, that was brilliant!" I sit on the toilet lid and lift my face so Becca can work some makeup magic.

"They're perfect together." Becca picks up a tube of concealer. "But I was afraid she'd say no."

"Who could say no to Buggy?"

"I got the idea when you told me Major was gone and that your grandmother seemed depressed." Becca smooths cream on my cheek. "I remembered how much she liked Buggy. I talked it over with Mom and the sheriff, and got the okay. A lot of the other pugs are finding homes too since the TV news reports. People from all over have called about adopting them."

Becca orders me to close my eyes, and I feel the brush of mascara and eye shadow. When she says I can open my eyes, I watch her apply dusky-brown eyebrow pencil and a smear of cinnamon pumpkin lip gloss.

With my hair and makeup done, I'm ready for the dance.

When the doorbell rings, I peek out to see Leo. I suck in a nervous breath. Will he like my hairstyle? Will he think my makeup is too much?

I open the door. He stares, his mouth dropping slightly.

"Wow," he says, which is so un-Leo-like.

"Come on in," I say, checking out his more-formal-than-usual look. He's wearing a long-sleeved white button-down shirt and a black tie instead of a vest. I like the look, and wonder if he'll hold my hand. I mean, he has to for dancing…right?

Trevor arrives too, and Becca grabs him by the hand and introduces him to Gran Nola and Buggy. While they're busy, I sit beside Leo on the couch. There's an awkward silence.

"Um…Becca gave Buggy to Gran Nola," I tell him.

"Can she do that?"

"The sheriff said it was okay."

"That's great." Leo pulls a pen from his pocket and twists it in his hands but doesn't say anything else.

"My parents have been house hunting, and Mom

says they've found one they like," I say, trying to make things normal between us.

He nods with more pen twisting. That's when I notice *what* pen he's holding—the poly-truth pen.

"Can I ask you something?" I ask like I'm a spy questioning a suspect.

"Sure." His truthful reply flashes green on the pen.

"When you asked me to the dance, was it because you just wanted to go to the dance or because you wanted to go to the dance with me?"

His eyes widen like a scared deer caught in bright beams.

"Um...I just thought a dance could be fun." A red flash.

I raise my brows. "So it's not a date?"

"Um...no." Another red flash.

This is kind of fun. I can't resist asking, "When the dance is over, will you want to kiss me good night?"

"Of course not." He blushes brighter than the flashing red pen.

"Good to know," I say, smiling.

From the living room, I hear a shout, "Chauffeur's here!"

I reach out for Leo's hand, and he hesitates, then grasps mine. Very much like a date, except that I sit up front with Dad, and Leo is in the back with Becca and Trevor. Minutes later, we're on the way to the dance.

While we ride, I notice that my father seems unusually excited, like he's bursting with news. It doesn't take much urging before he spills.

"Your mother wanted to wait till the papers were signed to tell you, but I can't hold it in any longer." He turns to face me while at a red light.

"What?" I strain forward in my seat belt.

"Our offer on a new house was accepted!" he exclaims with a huge grin. "We're buying a home!"

"A new house!" I bounce in my seat. "When can we move in? Do I get my own room? Does it have a big yard?"

"Whoa, Kelsey." He chuckles. "It's vacant, so we should be able to move in as soon as the papers are signed. You'll have more than your own room. Each of you kids can have a suite of your own. It's amazing! Three stories on five acres and right by the river!"

Something about this sounds familiar.

"Did it used to be a bed-and-breakfast inn?" I ask uneasily.

When he nods, I'm stunned.

"We're moving into the Down the Rabbit Hole B and B?" My hands fly to my face. "It's a huge, amazing house, but how could Mom want to live there? I mean, she was locked in that bomb shelter."

"It was her idea. She and I have always dreamed of running a bed-and-breakfast where I can be a chef in my own house." He pauses. "But there is one thing that's unusual—the house comes with an inheritance."

"What kind of inheritance?" I ask.

Dad shrugs. "We'll find out when we get the keys to the house."

"So it's a mystery?" I ask excitedly.

"I guess you could say that." Dad chuckles.

I grin and glance into the backseat where Leo and Becca are grinning too.

Another mystery for the CCSC!

I can't wait!

ᴀbout the Author

At age eleven, Linda Joy Singleton and her best friend, Lori, created their own Curious Cat Spy Club. They even rescued three abandoned kittens. Linda was always writing as a kid—usually about animals and mysteries. She saved many of her stories and loves to share them with kids when she speaks at schools. She's now the author of over thirty-five books for kids and teens, including YALSA-honored the Seer series and the Dead Girl trilogy. Her first picture book, *Snow Dog, Sand Dog*, was published by Albert Whitman & Company in 2014. She lives with her husband, David, in the northern California foothills on twenty-eight acres surrounded by a menagerie of animals—horses, peacocks, dogs, and (of course) cats. For photos, contests, and more check out www.LindaJoySingleton.com.